a horse called ELVIS

LEXILE™ 630

Scholastic Press
345 Pacific Highway
Lindfield NSW 2070
an imprint of Scholastic Australia Pty Limited (ABN 11 000 614 577)
PO Box 579, Gosford NSW 2250.
www.scholastic.com.au

Part of the Scholastic Group
Sydney ● Auckland ● New York ● Toronto ● London ● Mexico City
● New Delhi ● Hong Kong ● Buenos Aires ● Puerto Rico

First published by Scholastic Australia in 2004.
Text copyright © John Heffernan, 2004.
Cover illustration copyright © Lore Foye, 2004.
Cover design by Lloyd Foye & Associates.

Reprinted in 2004 and 2005 (three times)

All rights reserved. No part of this publication may be reproduced or transmitted in any form or by any means, electronic or mechanical, including photocopying, recording, storage in an information retrieval system, or otherwise, without the prior written permission of the publisher, unless specifically permitted under the Australian Copyright Act 1968 as amended.

National Library of Australia Cataloguing-in-Publication entry
    Heffernan, John, 1949–.
    A horse called Elvis.
    ISBN 1 86504 610 8.
    I. Foals - Juvenile fiction. I. Title.
A823.3.

Typeset in Espirit.

Printed by McPherson's Printing Group, Victoria.

a horse called ELVIS

by John Heffernan

A Scholastic Press book from Scholastic Australia

JUV.
PZ
7
.H3584
Hor
2004

To Elvis, the horse who became a mate.

JH

Prologue

*Things hang around in your head for years,
like old photographs in an album. Or old books in a box.
Faces and feelings gather dust at the back of your mind
and you seem to forget about them. But you don't.
The album falls opens one day—or you come upon
a box—and it's all there again, crisp and clear.*

*I'm going through things I don't use any more, boxes
of old toys and books. A photograph album.
There's a photo of me and a gangly foal only a few
weeks old, his eyes startled and red from the flash.*

*Who is he, this horse called Elvis?
The simple answer is that he's just a six-year-old
liver chestnut that I've grown up with. But there
is another answer, one that includes Nick, Jaz,
Mum and Dad. And me.*

chapter one

Right through the cruel, freezing night she stood in the same spot, resting one leg, then another. Even when the sun crept over the faraway hills, she still didn't move, waiting for the weak warmth to grow. In the early morning sun she cast a long shadow. It lay next to her like another horse. She wanted to lie down like that other horse, and might do so later in the day, when the sun had climbed higher and her body had thawed. But for now she stood statue-stiff, knowing that if she sank to the earth she might not get up again.

A dusty white truck had dumped her in the night. A tangle of wires and old wooden posts kept her in. A dead tree kept her company, along with several rolls of rusty wire, a scattering of builder's rubbish, and a cracked wrought-iron bathtub. The bathtub had once lived in a fine house, but was no longer of any use.

In a corner of the paddock where the ground sloped away, a hole had once been scraped to collect water. A shrunken brown puddle now lay there like a scab. Only when the horse became very thirsty did she make herself drink.

'Why?'

'Jeez, Matty, you're gunna really get it in a minute.'

'Yeah, but why?'

'Just get a move on, will ya?'

A girl and two boys straggled along a dirt path that bordered one side of the mare's paddock. The girl was older than the boys, and strode ahead. Before she turned off the track onto the side road into town, she hitched her school dress a little higher and lit a cigarette, sneaking a glance back at her brothers. They saw nothing.

'But why couldn't she?'

The mare heard the voices. Her ears flickered and she lifted her eyelids. The taller boy walked ahead, hurling words over his shoulder.

'You know why, Matty! She had to go to work early.'

'What about Dad, then?' the little boy's voice dribbled like a leaky tap.

'What about Dad?' the bigger boy snapped.

'He was doin' nuthin' this morning.'

'He's always doin' nuthin'. Anyhow, you know what Dad's like. You wouldn't want him to come.'

'Would too.'

The small boy stopped. In one hand he clutched a dog-eared picture book. Over his other arm hung his backpack. It was the only new thing on him. His shoes had come from his brother. They fitted, but the stitches were going and the heels badly worn. His shorts were too big, hoisted high around his waist with a belt. His shirt had several patches, and his school hat hung over his ears.

He let his backpack tumble to the ground and gazed at the picture book. The book was bent and worn, sticky-taped where it had been torn. The cover— with its picture of a boy sitting on a beach—was faded and cracked.

My picture book was about an island with crunchy crisp sand, palm trees nodding, white birds wheeling above a diamond-coated sea.
It was where I wanted to be.

'Come on, Matty. You'll be right. School's not that bad. You like Miss Barnett, you told me so.'

Matt pulled a face and looked away.

'Matt!'

The small boy turned to his brother for a moment, then gazed across the paddock towards the twisted tree, and saw the brown horse staring back at him.

'Pick up your bag and get a move on. I'm sick of this.'

Matt didn't pick up his bag. Instead, he climbed through the rickety fence and walked across to the horse, his book pressed to his chest. Nick called again, but Matt took no notice.

The mare watched the boy all the way. She stood as still as night, ears flickering, long nose stretching out to greet him. When Matt reached the old horse, he stood for a moment, staring at her. Large cracked hoofs in need of trimming. Spindly legs, bulging belly, ribs and hips protruding. Rough, dull coat, matted mane, huge head with big dark eyes.

He held out his hand, his fingers touching her mouth. It was soft.

Like mist from the sea.

The horse let the boy smooth his fingers over her rubbery lips. She lowered her head, letting the fingers explore further, creeping along the edge of her lips and up to her nostrils. She sniffed the fingers, and then the palm when the boy offered it. She gave a snort that startled him. But he didn't pull his hand away, and the mare continued sniffing, down his arm, across his chest, and up to his face.

'What are you doing, Matty?' The bigger boy had climbed through the fence and was standing next to his brother. He spoke quietly now. Matt didn't reply, but passed Nick the book so he could feel the mare with both hands.

'We gotta go, Matty. Can't be late again. It'll be the third time this week.'

'What's her name?'

'Dunno.' Nick placed his hand on Matty's arm.

'We'll have to make our own name for her,' Matt said.

'We'll do that.' Nick tugged at his brother's arm. 'We'll think of one on the way to school, eh?' The small boy didn't budge. 'Come on, Matty, please. Mum'll really crack if I get you to school late again, and then Dad'll make me work on Turbo all weekend.' He tugged harder, and eventually Matt allowed himself to be pulled away.

'See you later,' Matt whispered to the horse. 'After school.'

The horse watched the two boys walk away. They climbed through the fence. The bigger boy grabbed both bags and flung them over his shoulder. Then he passed the book back to his brother and took hold of his hand. The mare heard them laugh, and saw the small boy glance back, waving with the book before they disappeared from view.

When they had gone, she took a few steps.

chapter two

Matt inched his way through the backyard, tearing up grass and stuffing it into a hessian sack. The lawn had not been mown in ages. Nick and his father were on the other side of the privet-smothered post-and-rail fence that surrounded the house and garden.

Nick sat at the steering wheel of an old, mainly purple car, door open. His father was bent over the engine.

'Hit her again,' the father yelled.

Nick leaned forward and held two pieces of wire together. The engine groaned.

'Pump it a bit, for Chrisake,' his father shouted above the noise. Nick pressed his foot hard on the accelerator. The engine continued to splutter. The man poked his head around the side of the car, running his finger across his throat like a knife. The boy let the two strands of wire fall from his hands.

'Blowed if I know,' Ray Turner muttered, standing back and scratching his head with greasy fingers.

Two dogs watched from the back verandah. Guts was impossibly thin, despite the fact that he ate voraciously. TriHard, like the rickety table next to him —covered in dirty coffee mugs, empty beer bottles and two overflowing ashtrays—had only three good legs. He'd lost his fourth paw in an argument with a passing truck. A bent Coca-Cola can was now strapped in its place.

The verandah surrounded the house. It was wide and mostly safe, although some boards were rotten. The entire south side was stacked with old timber, broken window frames, piles of bricks and tiles, several boxes of nuts and bolts, and a bucket of bent nails.

The cobwebbed frame of a motorbike leant against the wall on the north side, and a hammock hung between two posts. Any remaining spare spots were filled by a straggle of old seats and armchairs. The dogs sat on two of these at the back of the house, watching everything that went on in the yard, day and night.

'It's not gunna go, Dad,' Nick said. 'Give up.'

The man stared at the boy. 'Ray Turner never gives up.'

'You reckon?' The boy rolled his eyes at the several

wrecks that lay between the post-and-rail fence and the mare's paddock.

'Spare parts,' Ray said. 'A treasure trove of spares.'

'I thought they were just junk.'

'Very funny. Any idea what you pay for a distributor cap for a Datsun 180Y these days? Or a fuel pump for a '75 Fairlaine?' Ray reeled off a list of car parts as he gazed over the gathering of auto skeletons.

He was a small man with a hard, stubble-covered face. His thin lips sometimes smiled, revealing two missing top teeth lost in a fight. But his mouth was more often kept tightly shut. His eyes could smile too, but not so often lately. There were two rings in one ear, and his wispy hair was pulled back in a ratty ponytail. Part of a tattoo was visible on his right arm, poking from beneath the sleeve of his T-shirt.

'In fact, that Fairlaine is closer to ready than you think,' he went on. 'A few finishing touches and she'd be rolling.'

'Like Turdo,' Nick muttered.

'Turbo will be purring like a bought one by the time I've finished.'

'Sure, Dad.'

Matt continued pulling up tufts of grass, drawing closer to the side gate. The sack was nearly full, almost as big as the boy himself. He stopped at the gate and called across to his father.

'You made that car go last year, Dad.'

Ray Turner nodded. 'The EH? She was a ripper.'

'Went for nearly three days,' Nick snickered, 'before she died of shock.'

His father pretended not to hear. 'They don't make them like that any more.'

'They sure don't, Dad,' Nick continued. 'These days they make cars that go.'

Matt wished his brother would stop. It only made his father angry. Then there would be shouting.

The shouting was always there, even when you couldn't hear it. Waiting like a shark, lurking in the depths at the edge of the reef.
A dagger in the dark.

Ray shook a spanner at his son. 'Quit your smart-alec comments and try to help. Or I'll give you one.'

The father whacked the spanner into the palm of

his hand, fixing his son with a glare before bending over the engine again. Nick screwed up his face at his brother and pulled the car door shut. It gave a loud screech.

'And put some bloody oil on those hinges,' his father yelled.

The car door screeched back open. Nick rummaged in the tool box for an oil can, and Matt returned to his grass-pulling, pleased that at least this time the shouting had drifted away.

'Stuff you!' Matt's sister shouted from inside the house.

'Jasmine!'

Matt turned and gazed towards the house. It stood alone, just south of the small town of Werrawee. The front looked west onto a large field. About two hundred metres from the back of the house a small creek trickled alongside a busy main road.

We lived on an island, a lonely speck in the sea.
At night the lights of Werrawee shone in the
distance, like a faraway port, and the cars that
slipped past were fishermen returning.
The trucks were big ships cruising by.

Further south, a gravel track left the busy road, snaking back through scrubby timber until it passed the front of the house. There it shrank into the dirt path that ran alongside the old mare's paddock, before joining the new bitumen road that detoured into town.

'Get back here!'

The back door squealed open and Jasmine ran down the steps. She wore jeans, low on her hips, and a tight-fitting T-shirt that left her midriff bare. Her blonde hair flashed in the sun as she flicked it back. Her lips were painted and her face made up so that she looked older than her fourteen and a half years.

Matt's mother came to the top of the steps and shouted. 'You heard me!'

The girl kept running around the side of the house towards the front gate. Matt watched, crouching behind his sack of grass. His father pulled himself from the bowels of the car. Nick stopped oiling the door.

The woman glared. 'Do something! She's your daughter, too.'

Mary Turner was a small woman, stocky, with close-cropped, mouse-coloured hair. She could wither anyone with the iciness of her glare.

'Jasmine!' the man shouted. His voice was thick with threat, but not enough to stop the girl.

The front gate clattered shut, and her footsteps scrabbled on the gravel. A moment later she was running past the old mare's paddock. The man yelled again, but the girl didn't stop.

Jaz was swimming for her life. Through the bay,
past the reef, out into the darkest depths
she swam, thrashing as hard as she could.
I held my breath, sure that dark fins would
slice after her, or that tentacles from
the deep would drag her down.

The woman glared at the man. Then she turned and stamped back into the house. Nick pulled the car door shut. His father stood waiting. So did Matt. They all knew what would happen next.

Music exploded from the house.

'You ain't nuthin' but a hound dog . . .'

The man sighed, shook his head, and returned to the engine. Matt stood up, opened the gate and dragged his sack through.

chapter three

'Here, Copper.'

The old horse saw the boy coming. When he reached the fence, she watched him grapple with the hessian bag, trying to lift it.

'Give up, Matty,' the boy's father called. 'She won't last out the winter, mate. Got the big C.'

Matt continued struggling with the sack.

'Waste of good grass,' said his dad.

The boy dropped the bag three times, but eventually managed to haul it over the fence. The mare ambled towards him.

He called her Copper because she was the same colour as the old coins his father kept in a jar. 'Come on, Cop.'

The boy dug into the sack, pulling out handfuls of green and holding them up to the mare. She nosed the grass, then closed her lips around it. As she chewed, the boy tipped more grass onto the ground. Then he turned and climbed back through the fence.

The mare chewed unhurriedly. The boy soon returned, lugging a large bucket. Water slopped from it as he walked, and more spilt as he first tried to lift it over the fence, before shoving it under the loose wires.

'Now you won't have to drink mud,' he said. The mare sucked at the water.

Matt pulled an old hairbrush from his pocket and set to brushing her. He worked slowly from the front, rubbing her thin neck, taking special care of her tangled mane. Then he brushed her knobbly legs, pausing to inspect an old scar. It ran from the fetlock of her hind leg on the near side, all the way up to her rump. He brushed her deeply dipped back, down her bumpy spine. He felt her bony ribs with his fingers. The mare barely moved, even when he crawled underneath to brush her huge, drooping belly.

Hanging on the fence was a length of rope that Matt had found under the house, and an old towel. He fetched the rope and tied it around Copper's neck. He threw the towel over her back. The mare glanced sideways at him.

Matt grabbed at Copper's mane, taking a handful

of the thick hair, and tried to scramble onto her. But she was too big.

The mare had drunk most of the water from the bucket. Matt tipped out the rest, turned the bucket upside down and stood on it.

He reached up and over the horse's neck, taking hold of her mane again. He sprang as hard as he could, knocking over the upturned bucket, leaving himself dangling from the horse's withers. She stayed still as the boy wriggled and kicked until he eventually hauled himself onto her back.

The mare took a deep breath, her belly expanding beneath his legs, then slowly exhaled.

'Where will we go, Copper?'

She flicked her ears, cast a backward glance at the boy, gave a shudder that made him clutch at her mane, then lowered her head and went on eating the grass.

We went down to a bay where the water was soft and calm. I could hear the roar of waves on the distant reef, but the bay was quiet. She drifted along the beach, wavelets lapping at her hoofs, and I stared out across the rippled skin of the sea.

*

'What are you doing?'

Nick was grinning up at Matt. Copper was no longer at the fence, but standing under the lone dead tree, scratching her rump on one of its lower limbs. The towel had fallen from her back and lay at the fence with the hessian bag and bucket. The rope had come undone too. It trailed along the ground, with Matt still holding firmly onto his end.

'Don't let Mum see ya. She'll go off her head.' Nick scrunched up his face and made his voice sound cranky. 'Git off that horse, she'll say.'

Nick picked up the trailing end of the rope, retied it around the mare's neck, and took the other end from his brother. 'Hang on, Matty,' he said, and began leading the old horse. She plodded behind him, nodding her head, her eyes almost shut.

Nick led us right into the bay. We waded out through the shallows, and further, the water lapping at Copper's side, creeping over my feet, ankles, knees, until it reached my thighs. We were a raft, with Nick at the helm, slipping silently out to sea.

chapter four

'Aren't you guys ready yet?'

Ray Turner stood at the kitchen door, covered in grease, with a big toothless grin. He'd been up since his wife left for work early that morning, tinkering with Turbo. Nick and Matt were at the kitchen table. Nick had finished his breakfast, but Matt had been feeding Copper, and was running late.

Neither of them needed to ask why their father was grinning. He had Turbo going at last. They could hear the car rumbling outside.

'She still wants some fine tuning,' their father explained. 'And the muffler needs fixing, but she's going! Eh, Nick? What'd I tell ya?' He ruffled his older son's hair.

Nick pulled away. 'We can walk,' he said. 'I've got to help Matt feed Copper, anyway.'

'I've fed her.' Matt shoved the last bit of toast into his mouth, unaware of the frown on his brother's face.

'Let's go, then,' their father said. 'Where's Jaz?'

'She left ages ago, Dad' Nick replied.

*

At Werrawee Central School a clump of girls hung on the fence behind the toilet block. On the other side of the fence two youths leant against a car. The car was a blotchy lime green with red and orange flames painted along the sides. It had two high aerials, each with a foxtail dangling from the top. The youths were smoking.

'Watch out for Dickson,' one of the girls warned. 'He's on the prowl.'

'So?' Jaz Turner smirked. She kept her eyes on the taller of the two youths. He was making smoke rings.

'Coming down the river this arvo?' he asked as the last smoke ring floated away.

'Might,' she replied. 'Aren't you working?'

'Night shift. Big kill on this week.'

'I'll be there,' said a smaller girl next to Jaz, throwing a quick glance at the other youth. He chucked his cigarette to the ground and stamped it out.

'What's going on here?' An elderly man appeared

at the corner of the toilet block. The other girls began to move away, but Jaz stared back at the man.

'Just talking, Mr Dick . . . son,' she replied. There was a ripple of giggles.

'Come on, you lot,' the Principal said. 'You know it's out of bounds.'

He began herding the girls away, but Jaz didn't move.

'You too, Jasmine Turner.'

Jaz would have stood her ground, but just then a loud rumbling noise was heard and a purple car spluttered around the corner.

'Aw, no,' Jaz muttered.

The roar was deafening as the old car struggled past the school grounds. Even so, everyone could hear the boy shouting.

'Jaz!' Matt yelled. He was standing up on the back seat, leaning across his father, head out the front window. 'Dad got Turbo going!'

But his grin fell away when he saw Jaz's horrified expression and felt his father's shoulders stiffen.

*

There was shouting at the house that night. Late, after Jaz got home. Mainly the father shouting at the daughter but, after that, the parents shouting at each other.

The sharks were snapping. They leapt from the depths, jaws wide open, yellow razor teeth, the sea frothing with their frenzy.

Matt sat on his bed, the island book next to his pillow, another open in his lap. Nick had brought a book home from the library. A picture book about mythical horses. Matt stared at a horse with wings. A young warrior was riding the horse, reining it in with one hand, a spear in his other, a shield slung over his back.

Across the room, Nick lay on his bed reading a magazine, trying to keep out the shouting.

Monsters slithered from the surging sea, tentacles rising, wriggling, writhing.

'Where the hell have you been?' Ray Turner bawled, his gruff voice pushing through the walls.

'Nowhere!' Jaz replied.

'Smoking!'

'Have not.'

'I can smell you a mile off.' There was a pause and Nick looked up from his magazine, wondering if that was the end of it. 'You've been with that Green boy, haven't you?'

'No.'

'I saw you this morning.' The anger was growing in the father's voice. 'Think I'm blind? Hanging around the back of the school toilets like a . . . '

Matt reached out and touched the winged horse. He ran his fingers over its fierce head and flaring nostrils. He touched its sleek body, its flowing mane and wide powerful wings.

'You've been with him, haven't you? In his car!'

'Haven't!'

Matt touched the warrior, with his bronze breastplate and plumed helmet, the broadsword slung at his side, the sharp spear. He looked at the words.

'Nick?' Matt climbed off his bed, picking up his island book.

'In his car!'

'Ray! Leave her alone.'

'Keep out of this!'

'Hey, Nick.' Matt stood at his brother's bed.

Nick had his back to him, his pillow pulled over his ears, staring at the magazine. Matt reached out and tugged at his brother. Nick spun around.

'What?' he shouted.

Matt flinched back, clutching the books. For a moment Nick had almost looked like their father.

Nick saw the fear on his younger brother's face, and softened his voice. 'How's the book?' he asked.

'Good,' Matt replied, leaning forward again, though he could still see embers of anger in Nick's eyes.

'Some pretty weird horses in there, eh?' Nick added.

Matt turned the book around, showing his brother the page he'd been looking at.

Nick nodded. 'Bit like Copper,' he said.

Matt grinned, moving closer.

'Different colour, but,' Nick continued, inspecting the picture. 'And size. And this one's got wings.

'What's its name?' Matt asked. 'And what's that say?' He pointed at the writing.

His brother inspected the writing for a moment. He took the book and flipped through it. Then he sat upright on the bed, crossed his legs and beckoned to his brother. Matt quickly climbed onto the bed.

This time Nick's bed was our raft, as he read me
the story of the winged horse and the warrior.
The monster in the book was slain, but the
monsters in our house circled closer.

chapter five

Matt and Nick sat at the breakfast table. Their mother had left for work much earlier than usual. She forgot to kiss either of the boys goodbye. Jaz had gone soon afterwards, not even bothering with breakfast. Their father was still in bed.

Silence hung over the house. Nick fiddled with his cereal, poking the soggy shapes around the bowl with his spoon, occasionally staring up at his brother.

Matt's head was still filled with wings and warriors and fierce horses. Copper would be a warrior's horse, he decided, as he chewed on his toast. Starting today.

Nick stood up, grabbing his cereal bowl and spilling some of its contents as he slouched across to the sink. 'Better get a move on if you're coming with me,' he said to Matt.

'Not going to school.'

'Don't be stupid.'

'I'm gunna look after Copper. Make her big and strong like the horse with wings.'

'Matty! She's never going to be . . . ' Nick stopped himself. What was the point? 'Suit yourself.' He turned and left the kitchen.

Matt stayed at the table. He heard his brother clumping around the house; in the bathroom, bedroom, hallway, slamming the front door, crossing the verandah. Even when he heard the click of the front gate, he stayed at the kitchen table. He spread jam on another piece of toast and smiled to himself. How he would make Copper shine!

His father came into the kitchen. He didn't see Matt, but went straight to the kettle, coughing and scratching himself as he waited for the kettle to boil.

Matt wanted to laugh, but didn't dare. His father was wearing only underpants, his thin body white and hairy. Ray made a cup of coffee, slurped at it, then turned around.

'What are you doing here?'

His father's voice was flat. Matt stared at the rough stubble on his face, his messy hair, the bags under his eyes. Then he recalled the night before. The shouting. It had gone on for hours, long after Nick had finished reading to him. Jaz had fled to her room and locked her door. Matt heard her crying in the early hours of the morning.

'You should be at school.'

'Not going,' Matt said.

'Like hell!'

'Gunna fix Copper, Dad.'

In two steps the father was beside Matt. With a flick of his wrist he gave the boy a sharp backhand across the ear. 'Want to end up like me, do ya?'

Matt yelped like a puppy and leapt up, holding his ear and bursting into tears.

'If you're not out that door in five seconds, boy, I'll give you something to really howl about!'

Matt ran from the house clutching his school bag, out the front gate and along the path that passed the old mare's paddock. Through his tears he noticed that the horse was lying down. He wanted to stop, but dared not. He called to her.

The mare didn't move and Matt hurried on.

*

'He's fourteen hands and has a blaze down the front of his nose. Dad says he's one of the best young horses he's ever seen. And I'm taking him to pony camp this year.' The boy stood in front of the other children, telling them his news for the day. 'His name is Lightning.'

'That's very interesting, Simon,' said the teacher. 'So your father has quite a few horses?'

'About ten, I think,' Simon Croft replied. 'We've got a new foal, too. Just born. We've called him Gonzo. Dad says he can be mine if I want.'

'Who else rides?' Miss Barnet asked the rest of the class. A forest of hands sprouted.

'I ride a motorbike,' one boy told the teacher.

'Me too,' several others added.

'She means horses,' a girl corrected them.

More children called out. Matt watched them clamouring. He wanted to tell the teacher about his horse as well. But it was too scary. The children always snickered whenever he showed Miss Barnett his island book. She's already seen it, they laughed.

Even so, before he knew what he was doing, his hand was in the air.

'Listen to you all,' the teacher said. 'Like a lot of monkeys. I can only see one good person.'

Matt realised he was that person. He quickly withdrew his hand, but it was too late.

'Matt.' Miss Barnet was looking at him. Everyone was looking at him. 'You have a horse, do you?'

Matt nodded, but said nothing. His face felt hot.

'Does he have a name?'

Matt nodded again, then shook his head. The whole class laughed. Matt's face felt even hotter. 'She's a girl horse,' he said eventually.

'A mare,' Simon yelled. 'We've got heaps of mares.'

'What's her name, Matt?' the teacher asked.

'Copper, Miss.'

'She's really old,' another boy called out.

'That doesn't matter, Nathan,' the teacher replied.

'She's not really his horse anyway,' Nathan continued.

'She is too!' Matt suddenly snapped.

'Someone just dumped her in the paddock near his house,' Nathan laughed. 'She's nearly dead.'

'Is not!' Matt shouted.

Nathan kept talking. 'She can hardly stand up. Just plods along.' Nathan stood and lolloped between the desks. 'Looks like a donkey. Heehaw!'

*

'I told you before, Matty. If you're gunna fight, you gotta get in early. Especially when they're big. Nathan Curry is a whale. You're just a shrimp.'

Matt and his brother were on their way home from school. They stopped so that Nick could wipe his brother's bleeding nose again.

'Don't wait for them to hit you. Or it'll be over before it starts.'

Matt flinched as his brother rubbed.

'Jeez, Matty! You're a mess.'

Matt shrugged. His nose hurt where Nathan had punched him. His knees and elbows stung from falling on the gravel, and his head ached.

Nathan had been waiting outside the school with his mates. They'd poked fun at Copper, heehawing and hobbling. Everyone in the bus lines laughed. So Matt had pushed him in the chest, then punched him.

'You idiot.' Nick finished wiping Matt's nose. 'All over a silly old horse.'

'She not a silly old . . . '

'All right, all right!' Nick jumped back. 'Don't hit me!' He laughed and threw his arm around his brother's shoulders. 'Come on. Let's get you home and cleaned up before Mum sees you.'

Matt saw Copper as soon as they turned the corner into the lane. Even from that distance, he knew. She was in the same place as she had been that morning. He dropped his school bag and ran.

All the signs were there—the crows that scattered like thieves, their lazy wails hanging in the air; the stillness of the mare; her legs poking out stiff and hard. The flies.

Matt scrambled through the fence and fell on his knees at her side. He squeezed his eyes shut as tight as he could, his face twisted, teeth clenched. Not Copper. Not dead.

'Matty.' Nick was standing behind his brother.

'No!' Matt pressed his fists against the horse's lifeless hide, his body buckled over the mare. 'Not fair!'

'Matty! Look!'

Matt didn't want to hear. He felt his brother's hand pressing on his shoulder, but shrugged it off.

Nick knelt beside him. 'Just have a look, will ya!'

Matt pulled his hands away from the horse, not wanting to feel the cold hardness. He pressed them against his face, trying to keep out the smell, against his ears to keep out the crows. Against his eyes.

Nick shook his brother and shouted. 'Open your eyes!'

At last Matt opened his eyes, but only because his brother wouldn't stop shaking him.

chapter six

'Stay right here. I'll get Dad.' Nick took a few quick strides in the direction of the house, then stopped. 'No, I'll get Mum. No, I'll get them both.'

Matt had never seen his brother so excited, shaking and smiling and serious all at once.

'Just stay here, okay?' Nick started running this time, but stopped again after only a few steps, looking back at his little brother for a moment before finally dashing off towards the house.

Matt leaned forward and peered at the brown bundle curled next to the dead mare's belly. A foal. Still covered in afterbirth, smeared with a mix of yellowy dried skin and old blood. The mare had not even managed to clean her foal before she died.

The boy reached towards the tiny creature, leaning over the mare. She made a sound when he pressed against her, a long groan. For a moment Matt thought that she might've still been alive. But she wasn't. It was just air escaping. The sound made the foal move. It gave a little shudder, but that was all. Then the boy touched the foal.

'What are you talking about?'

Matt could hear his father's voice drifting closer. And then his mother's.

Jaz was there too. 'What's so important that we all have to come?' she grumbled.

Matt heard the excitement in Nick's voice as he hurried them across the yard and through the fence. But Matt didn't turn around. His fingers were gently exploring the foal. Its body trembled with little flickers of life, then its head moved slightly, and its eyes opened, staring sleepily at Matt's fingers.

Matt's father stood beside the mare. 'Bloody hell!' The foal flinched.

'Oh, my God!' Matt's mother gasped.

Jaz immediately dropped to her knees beside Matt and reached towards the baby. 'It's so cute.'

The foal watched Jaz's fingers as she held them under its muzzle.

Mary Turner groaned and shook her head. 'That's all we need. What on earth are we going to do?'

'We're going to keep it,' Matt said.

'Don't be silly,' his mother replied.

'Copper left it for me, Mum. I've gotta look after it.'

'There's no way we can look after it!'

Matt glared up at his mother. 'I'm keeping him!'

Mary turned to her husband. 'Talk some sense into him.'

'Me and Jaz could help, Mum,' Nick said. His sister nodded.

'You two keep out of this,' the mother snapped. 'Ray!'

The whole family looked at Ray. He stared down at the foal, rubbing the stubble on his chin.

'Your mum's got a point, Matty,' he said. 'It'll be a real handful.'

'That's right,' his wife said.

'Its mother's dead, mate. We've got nowhere to keep it. No idea how to feed it or look after it. We wouldn't know where to begin. It could all end up a disaster.'

Matt gritted his teeth and stared back at his father.

Ray drew breath and scratched his head. 'Then again,' he added, avoiding his wife's eyes. 'Maybe we could . . . '

Mary turned and walked away.

Ray called after her. 'Just for a while.' She kept walking. 'Mary!'

The mother spun around. 'Who's gunna pay for the rotten thing? Vet's bills, vaccinations, feed. Not you, that's for sure!'

Ray shrugged his shoulders. 'We'll find a way.'

'You find a way, then.' Mary shook her head and strode towards the house.

Ray stared after his wife, then turned back to the children where they crouched around the foal. Matt sat with its head cradled in his lap, the foal trembling and watching the people with widening eyes.

'Right,' Ray said. 'Let's get this little feller up, then.' He leant down next to Nick 'We'll take the back half. Jaz, you help Matty.'

The foal flicked its head sideways as the hands gripped tighter, its eyes suddenly filled with fright. It wriggled, poking out its long front legs, trying to get up. It was heavier than they realised, and surprisingly hard to grab. It tossed its head and twisted its body. Nick tried to hold its hindquarters, but the foal kicked out and knocked him off balance.

Suddenly the foal was on its feet. It wobbled on stick-like legs for a moment, bumped against Matt and Jaz, and scrambled across Nick as Ray made another grab at it.

Then the foal ran across the paddock towards Mary, where she had stopped by the fence, the others running in pursuit. It ran right up to her and buried its head into her dress, pushing between her legs.

Mary squealed, and tried to push it away. But the foal stuck with her, bumping her with its head again and again. She waved her arms at it, shouting. Everyone was shouting.

Suddenly Matt realised what was wrong.

'Stop!' he yelled.

Everyone stopped.

'Don't move,' he whispered. 'See what happened? The foal went to Mum because she was the only one not chasing it. Stay still, Mum.'

She lowered her arms, and after a moment the foal began to quieten too. It stood next to the woman and looked around at the others with big scared eyes.

Matt started edging towards the foal, carefully, one step at a time. It watched him, pressing against the woman, forcing her into the fence. Matt made soft, friendly noises as he crept closer. When he was near enough, he slowly stretched out his hand and let the baby smell him. Then he started gently stroking the foal—on the chin, the mouth, nose, neck, down its side. Matt's mother nearly spoke, but he stopped her with his eyes.

After he'd rubbed the quivering animal for a few minutes, Matt rested his arm over its flank. The foal pushed against him. Matt stepped back, leaving his hand on the foal, and waited for it to come to him. The foal tilted its head slightly, stretched its neck towards the boy, curling its mouth and sniffing, then took a step. Matt murmured softly, and moved away again. The foal took another step. Soon it was next to the boy, sniffing him all over.

chapter seven

'For a start you'll have to milk the old girl.'

Ray had called Mr Barry, the vet, that afternoon.

'Milk the dead horse?' Jaz exclaimed.

'That's right. This little bloke probably hasn't even had a drink yet. What he needs most right now is a big dose of his mother's milk. That first drink is really important, you see, because it contains colostrum. It's full of goodness, and that's where the foal gets its strength and immunity.'

The Turners watched as Mr Barry milked the dead horse. So did the foal.

The mare had flies swarming all over her, blood and other fluid oozing from her mouth and nose and rear end. A trail of ants trickled from her ear.

The vet tugged at her stiff teats and managed to extract about half a litre.

'It looks okay,' he said, inspecting the milk.

Mr Barry poured the colostrum into a bottle fitted

with a rubber teat. He tried to feed it to the foal, but the foal struggled, pulling away. Then the vet smeared a small amount of the liquid on Matt's fingers. The foal sniffed the boy's fingers, then licked them, and eventually allowed them into his mouth. Once the foal had the taste of Copper's milk, the vet slipped the rubber teat in beside Matt's fingers. Within moments the foal was slurping down the colostrum.

The vet smiled. 'Looks like you're his mother, mate,' he told Matt. 'I'll give you this powdered milk to go on with. Make sure you mix it exactly as I say. Not too weak, not too strong. You'll make him sick if you do the wrong thing.'

'How often do we feed him?' Mary asked.

'That's the hard part,' the vet replied. 'Foals drink about every hour.'

'Thirstier than me, eh?' Ray grinned at the kids.

'For the first few weeks they drink all the time from their mums,' the vet said. 'Day and night. Only little drinks, mind, but all the time.'

Mary moaned. 'You're joking! How on earth will we manage that?'

'With difficulty,' Mr Barry replied. 'Someone has

to be with the foal most of the time in this early stage.'

'We can take turns,' Matt said. Nick nodded.

'Day and night?' Jaz asked.

'I'm afraid so. Someone will have to sleep with him, and have a bottle always ready. For a couple of weeks, anyway.'

'I told you this was crazy!' the mother scowled. 'And how much is this gunna cost, by the way? All up, I mean, rearing a foal.'

'Do you really want to know?' Mr Barry replied.

Mary shook her head and glared at the rest of the family, hands on her hips.

Ray shuffled uneasily. 'Not cheap, then, eh?' he said to the vet, avoiding his wife's eyes.

Nick and Jaz focused their attention on the foal.

Matt looked up at his mother. Her lips were thinner than ever and her eyes were like small black beads.

'It's got no mother!' Matt said. Mary looked away.

'What about the old mare?' Matt's father asked the vet. 'What do we do with her?'

'Got a crane and a truck?'

Ray shook his head.

'What about a tractor or something to dig a hole with?'

'Not really.'

'Got a match, then?'

'Yeah,' Mary Turner snapped. 'My bum and this bunch of losers!' She strode away.

*

Flames clawed at the night, splintered into sparks and then into nothing. Ray stood closest to the fire with Nick, kicking half-burnt sticks back into the flames. The mother watched from the verandah, Jaz from her bedroom window. Matt stood near the drooping fence with the foal beside him.

Ray and the children had collected wood from the paddock and stacked it around the mare. They'd taken rubbish from about the house and piled it over her. The foal followed Matt as they worked. Twice he had to stop and feed it.

By the time the pile was high enough, it was cold and dark. Ray poured diesel on the heap and lit it.

The foal stayed close to Matt as the fire took hold.

The boy's face was streaked with tears. His lips trembled, and every now and then his body shook with short, sharp gasps.

*My raft was breaking apart. I watched the sparks
rising through the night. Bits of Copper,
drifting away into a sea of stars.*

Matt felt the foal pushing against him. Its liver chestnut coat was red in the fiery light. The white blaze on its forehead glowed orange, its eyes were like small fires.

A tiny log bobbing in the water.

'You going to eat something?' Matt's mother had left the verandah and was standing behind him on the other side of the fence.

The boy didn't turn, partly because he didn't want his mother to see him crying, and partly because he wanted to keep his eyes on Copper's last moments.

He could barely make out her form deep within the flames. But despite the flames and the sparks, the smoke and the dark, and the strange smell of burning hide and bones, in his mind he saw her clearly. Large soft lips that quivered when he touched them. Long, friendly head poking down at him. Gentle, patient eyes.

'Matt.' His mother persisted. 'Do you want to eat or not?'

'Soon, Mum.'

He didn't want to confront his mother. There was still too much annoyance in her voice.

Matt's arm hung loosely over the foal's neck, his fingers tangled in its mane. 'We will look after him, Mum,' he said without looking at her.

His mother said nothing.

'We'll take turns feeding him.'

'Until you all lose interest.'

'No, Mum,' Matt insisted. 'It won't be like that.'

'Won't it?'

She stayed for a while longer, gazing towards the fire, then at the back of her son's head. He was gently stroking the foal's neck. Her tight lips relaxed a little. She turned and walked back to the house.

I pulled the log closer.

chapter eight

Ray slept with the foal that night. Mary refused to let Matt spend the night outside, he was far too young. But he and Nick sneaked down later when their mother was asleep. Jaz said she would join them, but in the end she stayed in bed.

There was a small shed at the bottom of the garden, where Ray stored spare parts. They cleaned it out as well as they could in the dark, shifting the bigger engine parts outside, stacking smaller pieces on the rickety shelves around the walls. Then they spread some mulching hay they had saved for the garden. It was mouldy, but it made a good bed for the foal.

The boys took their sleeping bags with them, as well as cushions from the armchairs on the verandah. Ray had collected some blankets and an old sponge-rubber mattress.

No-one slept much. The foal wouldn't lie down, but wandered back and forth sniffing things: the hay, the car parts, the people in their makeshift beds. Eventually he lay down, but he was soon up again and nudging at Matt. He didn't drink much, a few slurps at the bottle, and then he was sniffing and fidgeting again.

Once, when they did finally drift off to sleep, the foal knocked down one of the shelves, scattering car parts and startling everyone awake.

*

'Look at you lot!'

Mary Turner was at the doorway of the shed, staring in at the crumpled bodies. The foal stood in the middle of the shed floor, blinking at the morning light. Matt squinted out from his sleeping bag in the corner near the door. Nick was curled asleep near the foal on the rubber mattress and Ray was slumped in a car seat on the other side of the shed, head back, mouth wide open.

Matt's mother was in her uniform, ready for work, a camera in her hand. She shook her head and clicked her tongue. Then she held up the camera.

When the camera flashed, the foal wobbled on his spindly legs, stunned for a moment. He stepped backwards onto Ray's foot. Ray spluttered awake, startling the foal so that it leapt forward, clambering over Nick. Matt jumped up to try and calm the foal, but it stumbled past him and ran outside.

Matt was first out of the shed. He stood rubbing his eyes. Nick came next, yawning. Finally their father limped into the morning light. He paused in the doorway, inspecting his sore foot.

'What did you do that for?' he groaned to his wife. 'We were sound asleep.'

'Time you got up,' his wife replied. 'You have a foal to look after now. Remember?'

Matt headed after the foal. 'Look at him,' he called back to the others.

The foal was standing by the side gate of the post-and-rail fence, staring across to where the mare had been. A tangle of burnt wood lay in the middle of the paddock. Ray had thrown a couple of old tyres onto the fire before going to bed. A strip of smoke drifted lazily into the air.

Matt rested his arm across the foal's flank. The

foal looked at the boy briefly, then turned once more towards the smouldering pile.

Ray came hobbling across the backyard. He hadn't shaved for days, and stubble sprouted from his face like iron filings. Next to him, Matt's mother was fresh and neat in her uniform.

'What'll we call him?' Ray asked.

'Trouble,' his wife replied.

chapter nine

'Wop-bop-a-loom-bop-a-lop-bamboom!'

The foal turned his head towards the house and pricked his ears. He swished his tail at a horsefly and stamped his hoofs.

He knew this sound, for he'd heard it many times already over the last few weeks. Music blaring from the house—the twang of guitar, the rattle of drums, the piercing voice. The thump of people dancing, and sometimes laughter.

Ray straightened, stretched his back and leant against the hoe. 'Not the King again,' he muttered.

Mary had been playing Elvis Presley songs over and over for months. She'd taken up dancing lessons again. Therapy, she called it. Ray called it torture. He pictured her in there with the kids, twisting and jiving about and laughing. At least she was happy when she was dancing. He rubbed the small of his back where it ached, then continued with his gardening.

Ray was preparing a vegetable patch near the spare-parts shed. It was his way of helping with the bills, he told himself. The job had taken longer than he expected, the ground difficult to dig, the black soil sticking together in big clods. But it was almost finished. He'd worked at the soil until it was friable, raked in sheep manure and prepared most of the rows. He was finishing off the last of them now.

He'd have to fence the patch too, of course. Ray had already chased the foal away twice that morning.

The young colt sauntered towards the house, pausing to sniff at some garments hanging on the clothes line, then to inspect a beer bottle on the ground. He pawed at the bottle with his hoof, nudging it with his nose. The horsefly buzzed around his ears. He shook his head and moved on.

Soon the colt was standing at the bottom of the steps, where he was usually fed. He waited for the boy to appear, but all he could hear was the music and the noises coming from the house.

He placed one hoof on the first step. Then another. The hollow sound of his hoofs on the timber made him pause. He struck at the wood before moving to the next step, his front legs stretching out. Carefully he picked his way up two more steps and then leapt clumsily onto the verandah.

The two dogs lifted their heads. The foal eyed them, briefly sniffing at Guts, moving on when Guts growled. He wobbled past TriHard, pausing to nibble at his armchair, then picked his way around a cardboard box full of rubbish, still unsure of the hollow sound beneath his hooves. He stopped at the table with its broken leg, knocking off a coffee cup and sneezing when he sniffed one of the ashtrays. The horsefly landed on his rump, and he shuddered all over.

The music stopped, but the voices kept on. The foal edged his way past the table, past a pile of boxes and cartons, towards the window from where the voices came.

The music started again.

'You ain't nuthin' but a hound dog . . . '

The horsefly kept annoying the foal. The colt pigrooted, scattering several boxes. He reached the window from which the sounds were exploding.

The foal poked his head through the window, into the jumble of sounds and movement. The people were leaping around the room, twisting and turning and laughing.

Nick and his mother were practising a movement. 'You're the man,' Mary said, stopping for a moment. 'You have to take more control.' She grabbed his hand, spun him around several times and then pulled him closer. 'Like that!'

Nick took a firm hold of his mother's hand.

Matt and Jaz were partners. Matt was the girl, and Jaz was spinning him with one hand. He laughed as she twisted him around again and again until he was dizzy. Then he let go and stumbled across the floor, still spinning, his arms held out.

'I'm a helicopter!'

The sun slid down the waves and bounced across the bay. It shimmered up the beach, playing tricks on the flowers with the breeze. It flew among the birds and flirted with the trees.

The foal whinnied softly. He stamped his hoofs, shaking his head at the fly. His hoofs boomed on the verandah, and he whinnied again, louder.

'Look!' Jaz yelled, pointing towards the window.

Matt stopped circling. Nick let go of his mother halfway through a spin.

'He's dancing!' Nick shouted.

The horsefly landed on the foal's nose and stung him. The young colt scrambled backwards.

Matt and the others ran to the window. They laughed as they watched the foal twist and wriggle along the verandah, kicking and pigrooting. He jumped over one of the cardboard boxes and bumped into the table. The dogs scrambled from their armchairs and leapt off the verandah.

Ray heard the racket and stopped digging. He saw the table tumble over the edge, and the dogs scatter. The foal banged down the steps, then scampered about the house yard, rubbing his muzzle on the ground, wriggling and writhing.

'Hey!' Ray called to the faces at the window. 'Anyone who can jive like that has got to be Elvis!'

chapter ten

'Out here at once!'

Matt rolled over, clinging onto a dream. Soft mist on his face. Clouds drifting past like fine white hair.

'Now! Both of you.'

Matt peeped from under his blankets. His mother was standing in the doorway, glaring at him. He crawled from his bed.

'You too, Nick.'

The boys followed their mother down the hallway, past the kitchen, to the back verandah. Jaz and their father were there already, obviously just hauled out of bed too. The sun was poking over the distant hills.

'What time is it?' Nick yawned, rubbing his eyes.

'Stuff the time,' his mother snapped. 'Look!'

The two boys squinted. Clothes were strewn all over the back yard. A few socks and two towels still clung to the clothes line, as well a torn sheet. Scattered across the grass were shirts and underwear, shorts and school uniforms. A sheet had been dragged towards the vegetable patch, where it lay trampled and soiled. One of Mary's uniforms hung from the hedge near the side gate. Another lay under the clothes line, crumpled and filthy.

Standing at the bottom of the back steps, staring up at the people with a sock in his mouth, was Elvis.

Matt almost laughed, but Nick gave him a quick jab.

'I did that washing yesterday', Mary said, 'after I'd spent the whole day at work, cleaning up old people, making their beds, taking them to the toilet. I had planned to put my feet up when I got home, but I did two full loads of washing instead! No-one helped. Not one of you!'

Ray and the children stared silently at the chaos.

'I'm going to pick up my things. I'm going to wash them again at work. At least then I'll have somewhere safe to hang them. The rest I'll leave for you lot.'

'Don't worry, love,' Ray assured his wife. 'We'll look after it. Won't we kids?'

'You bet you will,' Mary said. 'But I haven't finished yet.' She glared down at Elvis. He was chewing the sock. 'That foal is nothing but trouble. I want something done about him!'

The sock had almost completely disappeared into the foal's mouth.

'Elvis!' Matt shouted. The foal stopped chewing. His ears flicked and he opened his mouth to whinny. The sock fell onto the bottom step, wet and crumpled. Matt glanced sheepishly at his mother.

'I've had enough of him wandering free,' she continued, 'chewing everything, digging holes, clumping up and down the verandah at all hours. It's been five weeks! I want something done with him!'

Matt held his hands up to his face. 'You mean get rid of him, Mum?'

'I didn't say that, Matty. But it's a warning. He's getting out of hand. He needs to be controlled.' She turned to her husband. 'Soon.'

*

Matt sat on the back step feeding Elvis. It was really Jaz's turn.

'No way,' she said. 'He went for me last time.'

She held out her hand, showing the bruise where Elvis had bitten her the day before.

'He bites us too, you know,' Nick told his sister, pointing to a mark on his arm. 'That's what foals do. You heard the vet.'

'We're like his mother to him,' Matt said. 'Foals often bite their mums, Mr Barry said so.'

'Just carry a stick and tap him on the nose,' Nick added.

Jaz shook her head. 'He tries to kick me, too,' she said. 'Anyway, I've got netball training.'

Elvis slurped at the milk, a white foam forming around the side of his mouth. He was drinking a whole litre now. Matt leaned sideways and stared at the foal's pot belly. Poddy animals always have bulging bellies, the vet told them.

'You're looking after him well, though,' Mr Barry had said. 'He's definitely growing.'

They'd established a roster system. After the first two weeks of almost constant hourly feeding, they gradually increased the time between meals. Ray fed the foal through the day. Matt fed him in the morning and after school. Nick gave him his final evening feed. Sometimes Ray added another at midnight.

Matt heard the hollow sound of the emptying

bottle, and pulled the teat from Elvis's mouth. The foal reached after the bottle with wrinkling lips. Matt rubbed him on the forehead.

'You *are* growing,' he said.

Nick and Jaz had already collected a pile of clothes each and taken them into the house. Matt's father was collecting the last stray socks.

'It's not good, Elvis,' Matt whispered to the foal. 'You're not meant to pull clothes off the line and chew them, or dig holes, or any of that stuff. Mum hates it. She said she mightn't even come home tonight!'

Elvis bumped Matt with his head. The boy threw his arm around the foal's neck and hugged him. Elvis was only doing what foals do—nudging and sniffing and chewing things to find out about them.

Matt pushed the foal away and slid the two railings into place that his father had set up to prevent Elvis climbing up the back steps.

Elvis sniffed the rails and then began gnawing at them.

Matt shook his head and laughed. 'You'd chew the moon if you could, wouldn't you?' He ruffled the foal's mane.

*

As he lay in bed that night, Matt tried to think how he could make things right with Elvis, so that his mother wouldn't be so grumpy.

He made himself stay awake, hoping that he'd hear her come home. If she *was* coming home. Jaz was playing music softly in her room. Nick rolled over and sighed. Matt heard his father pacing through the house. He heard Elvis's soft muffled call from the back steps, and then heard the foal paw at the railings.

Railings! Matt suddenly had an idea.

'Nick,' he whispered into the dark. 'We need a yard for Elvis.' There was no reply. 'A place to keep him in.' A gust of wind ruffled the bushes outside. 'That would make Mum happy!'

Nick stirred, but said nothing.

I felt the movement, and leaned over the edge of my raft, peering into the water. The sea was the colour of coal, and I saw nothing. But I felt it.

A slow movement far beneath, like some huge and shapeless thing stirring, pushing up the water, forcing it to swell about the raft like oozing oil.

A friend brought Mary home. Matt heard a car grind up to the house along the dirt road. He thought he heard a man's voice, just for a second, before the car door closed. He tried to think who it might be. But he was too sleepy. He let his fingers explore beneath his pillow until they found the island book.

'Where have you been?'

> *Rumbling in the distance,*
> *the sky slashed with light.*

chapter eleven

'Not much left of her, eh?' Nick said.

Matt stared at the chunks of charcoal, the stubs of half-burnt branches, the distorted form of a melted beer bottle, a shrivelled piece of horse hide, charred bones. His father had burnt more rubbish on this spot, and raked over the charcoal. Matt could still see the old mare's skull, her ribs and hip bones, but the rest was a scattering of blacks and greys, like an old photograph.

Nick prodded his brother. 'Can't stand here all day.' The bigger boy moved off, lugging a large roll of old wire. 'Got these yards of yours to finish.'

For the last two weeks the boys had been building a pen for Elvis at the back of the garden, just outside the post-and-rail fence.

Matt and Nick had discovered five wooden posts underneath some rolls of rusty wire in the old mare's paddock. They'd found a pile of old steel droppers too. The droppers were rusted and mostly bent, but they managed to straighten them reasonably well.

The rolls of wire were too rusty to use. So they pulled some wire from the rickety fence around the paddock—Nick said it wouldn't be missed—and coiled it into two rolls. Matt grasped hold of his roll and began dragging it in pursuit of his brother.

The boys were using the post-and-rail fence as one of the sides. Each day as they worked, Elvis watched from the old fence with its rambling hedge, or stood with his head over the side gate, neighing at the boys.

'Won't be long, Elvis,' Matt called back. 'Your very own yards.'

Their father had helped them lay out the plan for the pen. He'd also cut the post-and-rail fence to make a gateway from the garden into the pen. But then he lost interest. Nick dug the remaining holes and rammed in the wooden posts as best he could.

Knocking in the steel droppers had been the hardest part. Nick used a sledgehammer, while Matt tried to hold the posts steady.

'Stop wobbling them,' Nick had to shout at his brother more than once. 'It's hard enough knocking them in straight without you moving all over the place.'

'Dad could do it,' Matt replied.

'Yeah, but he's not here, is he?' Nick snarled. 'Just do as you're told. This was your idea.'

They used an old hand drill to make holes for the wire in the wooden posts. It seemed to take forever. But now that was done and they were ready to feed out the wire.

'I'll get Dad,' Matt said to his brother as he let his roll fall to the ground.

'Don't bother,' Nick replied, glancing towards the house.

They knew their father was slumped in front of television. They also knew that it was best to leave him alone. Ever since their mother came home late with her friend that night, Ray had grown increasingly sullen. What's more, Mary had taken up extra dancing classes in Grayston, heading off to the larger town twice a week. She came home very late on those evenings, and the parents' arguing filled the house on Wednesday and Friday nights.

'You and your bloody dancing. Dunno what you see in it.'

'You wouldn't.'

'Unless it's more than dancing, eh?'

'Leave me alone.'

'That's it, isn't it?'

'Just shut up!'

Nick grabbed his roll of wire. 'We can do it ourselves,' he said.

Nick pulled the wire through the holes, while Matt fed it from the rolls, trying his hardest not to let the wire kink. They put six lines of wire in the fence, the top one almost as high as Nick's chest, and then strained them by hand.

It was dark when they finished. The two boys stood in the middle of the enclosure, silently admiring their yards. They tried not to notice that the wooden posts wobbled, that the steel droppers were crooked, and that the wires were sagging and twisted.

'We did it, Nick. You and me.'

Nick nodded, and then whispered to his brother. 'Look.'

Elvis was approaching them. They stood still. He sauntered along the post-and-rail fence. When he reached the gateway he stopped and nudged the wooden posts, chewing at one of them, his teeth gnawing on the timber. He took a few more steps, pausing in the gateway to sniff the wires and the steel posts. He looked across at the boys, tilting his head sideways. Then he joined them, snuffling at Nick's pockets first, then gently butting Matt with his head.

Lights were on at the house—in the kitchen, the hall, Jaz's room. The girl's shadow paused at her window. The sound of the television drifted across the backyard.

'Let's hope it keeps him in,' Nick said.

chapter twelve

Mary Turner climbed into Turbo.

'Bye, Mum,' Matt called.

He stood with Elvis at the front gate and waved. It was Saturday and she was off to a special dance session. There was a competition, too.

'Show them what you're made of,' Nick yelled from the verandah.

Matt stared at his mother. She looked so beautiful when she went dancing. Lips bright red, eyes made up, hair soft and sparkling, her perfume hanging in the air. She was like another person—a princess—off to a castle somewhere in a coach.

Except that Turbo wasn't much of a coach. And where was her prince?

The car spluttered and backfired. Mary smiled at her boys. Then she saw the foal munching on one of her zinnias and frowned. She almost said something, but then decided not to. The boys had been trying: the funny ramshackle yards they'd built; the halter and lead rope they were saving up for.

She smiled again, pressed the accelerator, and waved goodbye. Turbo's oily blue exhaust hung in the air like a shadow.

Matt stayed at the gate, his arm around Elvis. Nick went straight to his room. When the sound of Turbo had faded, Matt gave the foal a hug, then left him and entered the house. Elvis stood on the path, staring at the front door for a moment, before stepping up onto the verandah.

As Matt walked down the hallway, he saw his father slouched in front of the television, although it wasn't on. The only noise he could hear was the whine of the vacuum cleaner from Jaz's room. He went to the kitchen, took Elvis's mixing jug from under the sink, and got down the canister of powdered milk from the cupboard next to the table. The vacuum cleaner stopped. The television started. It was louder than usual. Matt paused at the table and stared into the sitting room.

His father was still slumped in the armchair, but he wasn't looking at the television. He was staring at a can of beer in his hand, his lips pressed tightly together. He wrenched the can open. Then with his eyes shut, he jammed the can to his mouth and gulped until he'd almost emptied it.

He burped, wiped his face with the back of his hand, and raised his gaze to the television. Jaz's bedroom door closed.

'Jasmine!' Ray shouted without looking up, as his daughter passed the sitting room door. 'Where do you think you're going?'

'Town.' Ray turned towards the girl. 'Mum said I could.'

'Bit tarted up, aren't you?'

'No.'

'Cleaned your room?'

'Have a look for yourself.'

He didn't have a look. 'Be home by six or I'll come after you,' he snarled instead, lighting a cigarette. 'And I mean it!' His voice was swallowed by the empty hallway.

Ray dragged heavily on the cigarette, his eyes fixed on the empty doorway where his daughter had been. The front door closed, and the gate clacked. In his mind, Matt saw Jaz escaping down the dirt track. Then he realised that his father was looking at him.

'What are you staring at?' Ray growled. Matt held up the canister as a kind of excuse and hurried back to the kitchen sink.

Elvis heard the girl close the gate and walk away. He was on the northern side of the house, just around the corner on the verandah. He sniffed at some ivy that grew along the wall, then continued down the verandah towards the back of the house, pausing at the hammock and the cobwebbed motorbike frame. He turned the corner at the back of the house where the two dogs were lying in their armchairs.

The foal inspected Guts first, sniffing at the thin dog. Guts gave a low growl and the young horse pulled away. Elvis chewed the arm of TriHard's chair for a moment, then noticed the Coca-Cola can. He leaned forward. TriHard flattened his ears. Elvis nudged the can with his nose, then tried to bite it.

The dog sprang straight at Elvis and sank his teeth into the colt's nose. The foal stumbled backwards, slipping on the verandah boards and falling on his side. TriHard pounced on him, and Guts followed. Elvis tried to scramble up, but was knocked sideways off the verandah. He gave a sharp squeal as he hit the ground with a thud, legs thrashing at the air. The two dogs threw themselves from the verandah onto him.

Matt was at the kitchen sink, mixing Elvis's milk. He heard the racket and looked through the window in time to see the colt topple off the verandah, pursued by the dogs. He ran screaming from the kitchen.

By the time Matt reached the verandah, the colt was fleeing across the backyard pursued by the dogs. Matt ran after them, yelling, as the dogs chased the colt down to the back corner, leaping at his flank, snapping at his neck and rump.

Elvis swerved to escape them, crashing into the side of the spare-parts shed, the corrugated iron clattering loudly. Scrambling up, he stumbled into a pile of rubbish behind the shed. A strand of barbed wire tangled around his front legs. As he struggled, the wire dug into his flesh, tightening. He reared up on his hind legs, teetered sideways, and fell heavily.

Matt screamed, grabbing and hitting at the dogs. Elvis was squealing, hind legs kicking, front legs thrashing, barbed wire lashing at the air. Suddenly

Nick was there too, in amongst the tangle of snapping and snarling.

Then the father. His face was red and contorted. He shoved the boys aside and, grabbing a lump of wood from the pile of rubbish, fell upon the dogs.

The boys stared in horror as their father whacked into the dogs with the wood, screaming abuse. Guts ran off, yelping, but TriHard kept biting at Elvis. The man grabbed hold of the dog by the neck. He ripped him off the foal and hurled him as hard as he could across the yard. The Coke can fell off the dog's leg and he stumbled a few metres before collapsing.

Matt and Nick went straight to Elvis. The colt kicked out at them, and tried to bite. But Matt knelt amongst the rubbish beside the foal, gently stroking his neck while Nick began to untangle the barbed wire. Matt could feel the young horse's heart hammering, his body quivering. There were several deep gashes on his side and rump, his nose was bleeding, and his front legs were torn from the barbed wire.

The boys tried to ignore their father as they tended to the foal. Ray chased Guts all the way to the house, but the dog scrambled in amongst the rubble under the verandah. The man tried to dig him out, grasping at bits of timber and rubbish, tearing them out, swearing and shouting.

Nick worked carefully but quickly at the wire. The foal flinched and kicked. But eventually Nick loosened the wire enough to free Elvis's legs. He dragged the wire away from the shed towards the back gate, twisting it together into a bundle. Matt stood back to let Elvis jump up, but the foal stayed on the ground, panting and trembling.

Matt turned and saw his father loping back from the house. He'd given up on Guts, and was heading for TriHard. The dog lay cringing under a tree. The man pounced on him, holding him down, and started punching him.

It wasn't my dad. It couldn't be!
It was a monster that had crawled from the sea.

They were tangled together, the man and the dog, a single struggling creature. Their yells and howls mingled into one awful sound.

Nick dropped the wire, ran straight at his father

and grabbed hold of his sleeve, tugging at him, pleading with him. But the man kept punching. Nick clambered onto him and pulled his head back until the man finally toppled sideways. TriHard scrambled up and limped away.

Ray spun around. He seized Nick by his shirt, yanked him down and pinned him to the ground.

Matt stumbled from the foal's side. His legs buckled under him and he fell. He floundered on the ground, helpless as he watched his father raise his arm above his brother. He felt a howl within him clawing to escape.

Trapped underwater! Struggling in the deep.
Unable to surface, lungs bursting, legs kicking,
arms flapping, unable to scream
through the leaden liquid.

The foal had scrambled up and was running towards the tangle of man and boy. He circled them, limping, shaking his head, making strange squeaking noises. The man froze. He lowered his arm, and covered his mouth with his hand. He closed his eyes and muttered something. Nick rolled free of his father, stood up, and walked away.

Ray watched his son go, one hand still covering his mouth. He lifted his other hand, as though reaching towards Nick, but then thrust it to his mouth as well. His body slumped, and slowly he buried his face in his hands.

The monster hadn't crawled from the depths at all. It had always been on our island. Hiding amongst us. Waiting for the right moment to attack. Now it shrivelled away, leaving only a frightened little man in its place.

chapter thirteen

Matt sat on the corner of the front verandah, the afternoon sun warming him. Elvis stood nearby in the garden. Through a gap in the hedge, the boy watched Jaz talking to the youths and another girl. They were leaning against the lime-green car, twenty metres along the track.

The foxtails on the aerials waved in the wind. Matt smiled at the way the youths and the girls fooled about, enjoying their loose, free movements.

Then they all climbed into the car. The doors slammed, the engine revved a few times, the car spun around in the gravel and drove away down the dirt track to the main road, taking the laughter with it.

The front door opened and Matt's mother stepped onto the verandah, staring intently in the direction of the disappearing car. Her shoulders slumped slightly as she stood, one hand gripping the gauze door.

She was still wearing her work clothes, although

she'd changed her shoes for scuffs, and had thrown an apron over the blue and white uniform. She sighed. Elvis snorted, lowering his head to nibble at the grass. Realising she was being watched, Mary suddenly turned towards Matt.

Matt wanted her to smile. Wave to him. Say something friendly. But all she did was stare, her eyes tired, her lips set tight.

'Make sure you put the foal away tonight,' she eventually said.

'Yes, Mum.' The boy smiled expectantly up at his mother. He wanted to remind her of how things were getting better. How Elvis had only broken out of his yards once. How they now had a halter on the colt, and a rope to lead him around. How Dad had a job now, even if it was only two days a week, and how that would help pay for things. But before he could work out how to say all this, his mother had gone, the gauze door banging behind her like a full stop.

Matt stepped off the verandah and wandered down the side of the house. Elvis followed, bumping the boy in the back, and nibbling at his elbow with his velvety mouth. The colt lowered his head and poked it under the boy's arm, then let Matt climb up and lie across his back as the two of them continued past the house towards the pen.

More than three weeks had passed since Elvis was attacked by the dogs. The barbed-wire cuts on his legs were only marks now, and the wounds from the dog bites were clearing up, although the deep gash on Elvis's rump was much slower to heal. Matt ran his fingers gently over the wound and the foal's skin flickered.

The dogs lifted their heads and watched from the armchairs as Matt and Elvis passed the edge of the verandah. After his beating, TriHard had hidden under the house for days, not even appearing to be fed. Nick eventually coaxed him out and fitted a new Coke can onto his stumpy leg. Both dogs had now returned to their armchairs, but they still watched the man warily whenever he appeared.

Matt slid from Elvis when they reached the pen, and fetched some hay and oats from the spare-parts shed.

The boys never spoke of that Saturday afternoon. Not to Jaz. Not to their mother. Not even to each other.

The silence festered.

Matt unlatched the gate into Elvis's pen. The colt watched the boy enter, but didn't follow. He didn't like being locked up. Matt called him, but the foal stayed where he was until the boy held out some grain in his hand. He pushed the grain under Elvis's nose, whispering to him, then stepped back into the yards. The foal followed.

Matt brushed Elvis as the foal fed. 'Now you stay here tonight,' he said. Elvis tossed his head and snorted. 'No more pushing through the wires.'

The colt had already escaped once. Nick had pulled the wires as tight as he could, and so far the fence seemed to be working.

Matt filled the water bucket and gave the foal a hug. 'No milk tonight,' he whispered. They were gradually cutting it back. 'I'll give you a big bottle tomorrow morning.'

Elvis stared at the bucket for a moment, and then began drinking. Matt slipped quickly out of the pen, shutting the gate and flicking the latch into position.

He heard Turbo coming. Ray was returning from his first day at work in months. Mary had lined up a part-time job at the abattoir for him. Cleaning, two days a week.

Matt ran along the side of the house to the front gate. His father had just closed the car door, and stood staring at the ground.

'How did it go, Dad?' Matt called from the gate.

Matt's father remained staring, as though he hadn't heard. Then he looked up and gazed across at Matt.

'Fed the foal?' he asked.

'Yes, Dad. And I've locked him up.' Matt smiled at his father. 'Elvis's wounds are healing too. I checked them all.'

Ray opened the gate. 'Jaz home?'

Matt half expected his father might pick him up.

'No,' he replied as the man pushed past him. 'She's . . . '

He wasn't sure what to say. He remembered the foxtail aerials bobbing in the wind.

His father walked up the front path and went inside.

*

Elvis whinnied, ears pricked towards the house. The lights were shining. He'd whinnied many times, but no-one came. He pushed against the wires. He paced around the small yard, stopping to strike at the ground with his front hoofs, knocking his bucket over and prodding it along the ground.

Then he went to the gate. He fiddled with the latch, poking it with his nose, nibbling at it, finally letting his long tongue tease the metal piece. The latch slipped free. The gate swung open, the colt stepped outside and headed for the house.

Elvis paused at the steps. He listened for the woman with her broom. He nickered for the boy. He eyed the dogs. They'd been asleep but were now wide awake, watching him. Guts sat up and peered over the arm of his chair. TriHard lay low, his ears back.

The colt climbed the steps and was soon standing at the back door. A shaft of dull light shone from inside, and Elvis could hear sounds. He struck at the door with his hoof. It moved a little. He bumped it with his head, and it opened further, enough for him to push his muzzle through and enter.

Inside, the floor was soft and silent beneath his

hoofs. He paused at the kitchen door. It was shut, but Elvis could hear the people.

'I don't care,' said the woman's voice. 'It wasn't easy getting that job for you.'

And the man's voice. 'Don't worry. I'm not gunna chuck it in.'

'Wouldn't be the first time.'

'Jeez.'

Then the clinking of plates and glasses, footsteps, a chair being scraped along the floor. Elvis looked down the hall. It was dark, but a flickering blue light shone from a doorway. He walked towards it.

Elvis came to a room in which there was a box that gave off sounds and light. The colt moved closer until he was in the middle of the room. There he stopped and watched the flickering box, mesmerised by its shimmering glow. He could still hear the people through a second door on the far side of the room.

'There's talk of lay-offs, you know?' The woman again.

'I'll be the first to go, then,' the man replied.

'Not if you do your job properly. Remember that.'

The woman's voice grew louder, closer. The door

opened and light spilled into the room. The woman was standing in the doorway. She flicked on the sitting room light and stared at Elvis.

'That's it!' she shouted. 'Bloody horse!'

Soon the boys were standing next to her. Then the man.

Elvis's hooves were firmly planted on the carpet, his legs astride, his body long and stretched out, a dip in his back. Beneath him, a vast pool of liquid spread across the carpet. The long drawn-out whooshing sound was ended off by several short squirts.

'Get him out of here,' Mary whispered, trying to control her anger. 'Get him out before I get a gun!'

Matt and Nick heard their mother shouting as they led Elvis back to his pen.

'Mad house, pigsty, rotten hole. Working my guts out! Useless good-for-nothings! Can't stand it any more!'

Her abuse spewed from the house—louder, and with a sharper screech, than ever before.

'It's me and Elvis, isn't it?' Matt said as they reached the foal's yard. 'We're to blame.'

'Don't be stupid, Matty,' Nick replied.

Matt was shaking. 'If Elvis hadn't . . . '

'It's him this time. But if he hadn't pissed, it'd be something else. Mum is . . . ' Nick thought for a moment. 'I don't know.'

The two boys stood in the dark with the colt.

The black of night. People running, stumbling
in the sand, colliding, shouting but not hearing.
People in the water, crying for help.
No-one ever hearing. Only fear.
Clinging like wet sand.

chapter fourteen

Elvis peered after the boys, ears erect. He called. Waited. He paced the perimeter, tossing his head, and called again. He charged at the fence, swerving at the last minute, spun on his haunches and pigrooted.

'Come on, Matty.'

Matt glanced over his shoulder at Nick, then back at Elvis. The boys were earlier for school than usual. They'd left the breakfast table as soon as their father appeared, hurrying away, heads down. Matt still had his toast. He took a quick bite, then dropped his bag and ran back to Elvis.

'Matty!'

Elvis whickered as the boy approached. 'It's got strawberry jam on it,' Matt said. The colt leaned over the fence, sniffing at the toast. He delicately picked it up with his lips, lifted it, then let it fall to the ground.

Matt stooped to pick up the toast, but it was covered in dirt. He left it there. 'You'll be all right,' he said to the foal, rubbing him on the forehead. 'You have to be!'

The back door creaked open as Matt's father stepped onto the verandah.

'I've got to go.' Matt tickled the colt under the chin. Elvis pulled his head away. The boy turned and ran after his brother. The colt stood at the fence and watched the boys disappear.

Ray slurped at his coffee and stared down at the colt. Guts lay in his armchair, eyes on the man. TriHard had already left his chair. He stood at the far corner of the verandah, staring back at Ray, tail between his legs. Ray lit a cigarette and sucked hard on it.

The colt cantered back and forth in his pen, whinnying over and over. Ray tried to ignore him, but couldn't. He stubbed out his cigarette after a few puffs, gulped at his coffee, tipping the rest over the edge of the verandah, and turned to go back into the house. But the colt's distressed call nagged at his back. He glanced at his watch. Should have been at work already.

'It won't take long,' he told himself.

He strode quickly down to the spare-parts shed,

grabbed a small amount of hay and went to the pen. The colt stood back, eyeing the man warily. Once he might have gone straight to him and eaten from his hand. Not any more.

Ray waited, holding out the hay. He saw the fretting in the animal's eyes, the doubt.

'Come on, mate.'

He edged closer, shaking the hay and clicking his tongue.

'I won't hurt you.'

Elvis approached the man tentatively. He sniffed at the hay, nibbling a small amount, letting the rest fall to the ground. The man reached out to touch the colt, but the animal snorted and pulled away.

'You too,' Ray muttered.

He heard his wife's voice shouting in his head. He saw her face staring coldly at him, the sullen anger of Jasmine, the fear in Matt and Nick. He turned and left the pen, twisting the wire that the boys had added to keep the gate latch secure.

*

Even after the people had long gone, Elvis still paced the fence, whinnying. He tested the gate, but the latch was firm and no amount of nudging or licking would move it. So he pushed at the fence, pressing his chest against it, rubbing his side along it. He struck out with his hoofs, scraping at the wire, jabbing at the earth. All morning he jabbed and scraped and dug.

Gradually the colt was able to make a hole in the dirt. He kept working at it with his front hoofs until it became deeper. He scraped at the sagging bottom wire, loosening it even more. He dropped to his knees and forced his head under the wire, pushing upwards with his strong neck. The wire began to give, rising from the ground. He prised it upwards with all his might, twisting and wriggling in the dirt, until in the end he broke through.

Elvis stood up and shook himself, a flurry of dust rising into the air around him. He sneezed and wrinkled his nose. Then he shuddered all over, and stared about.

He was out in the open. With his tail arched and a slight dip in his back, he strode along the side of the privet hedge to the dirt track that ran past the front of the house. There he turned and followed the track in the direction the boys took in the mornings. He paused at the sagging fence and stared across at the dead tree and the mound of charcoal and bones. Beyond the paddock, cars moved back and forth along the main road.

Behind him, on the other side of the dirt track, was a large open field. Elvis turned, tipped his head into the breeze, sniffing briefly. Then he broke into a gallop, his front legs stretching out, his hoofs striking at the ground, sending clods of earth flying. A nest of plovers scattered as he thundered past, and a rabbit cringed next to a fallen log as the colt leaped.

A dusty white truck pulled off the main road on the other side of the old mare's paddock. It stayed there, idling, while the colt galloped and pranced.

Elvis spun on his haunches, headed back, and jumped the log again, this time sending the rabbit scampering. While still in the air, he twisted his body sideways and kicked out with his back legs. He continued to kick as he galloped off, doing wide circuits of the field, jumping logs and ditches wherever he found them.

As quickly as he had started, Elvis came to a sudden halt. He stood still, his body warm now, ribs and flank rising and falling. Chest out, head high, the blaze on his forehead like a streak of lightning, Elvis returned to the dirt track with neat, high paces.

The white truck pulled back onto the main road and drove along to the turn-off into Werrawee.

Elvis stood on the hard black road that led into town. He heard yelling and laughing in the distance, children's voices, and headed towards them. He didn't notice the truck creeping along well behind him.

He followed the road between the rows of houses until he came to the school. The grounds were now empty and quiet, although the colt could hear faint voices coming from a collection of buildings. He walked along the boundary until he found a gate, and wandered into the school grounds.

The young horse was hungry, so when he came to a vegetable garden he stepped over the low fence. He walked along a row of cabbages, nibbling at a few, trampling others. He crossed to a row of brussels sprouts, plucking some from the ground, nodding at their sweetness as he munched.

Two men watched from the truck parked under a tree near the toilet block.

*

When Mr Dickson called Matt from his class, the boy knew something was wrong. The Principal's face was puce and he could barely speak. Nick and Jaz were with him, their faces red. For a moment Matt thought something terrible must have happened at home.

'Follow me!' Mr Dickson said and strode down the hallway.

'It's Elvis,' Jaz hissed at Matt as Mr Dickson lead the three Turners outside.

'What's Elvis?' Matt asked.

'What's Elvis?' Mr Dickson exploded. He spun around and stared down at Matt. 'He's a disaster area, that's what he is.' They were halfway across the quadrangle. 'He's a four-legged hurricane!' He turned and pointed towards the school's horticultural plot. 'A *tsunami!*'

Elvis was standing next to a small greenhouse, chewing. The glass was broken where he'd leaned against it. He looked up, saw Matt and whinnied, a piece of cauliflower tumbling from his mouth

'Your sister informs me that you are the only one who can control this . . . creature,' the Principal said to Matt. 'Do it, young man. Now!'

As the Turner children led Elvis home, they didn't notice the truck trailing them. Nick and Jaz were laughing. They'd never seen old Dickson so flustered. Matt laughed too, but not as much. He was too worried, huddled in his thoughts. How would they tell their mum? What would she say? What would she do?

When they turned off the road onto the dirt track, the truck stopped opposite. An elderly man hung his elbow out the window and peered after the children and the foal.

'Not a bad looking colt,' he said.

'Plenty of spirit,' the other man added.

'Plenty of jump, too.' The man at the window kept his eyes on Elvis as he clunked the truck into gear.

The other man's words were swallowed by the engine's roar. The truck drew away from the curb, chugged the short distance to the main road, then turned towards Grayston.

chapter fifteen

'Keep pulling, will ya!'

'I am!'

'Pull harder, then!'

'I can't!'

Matt slumped onto the ground, exhausted. The two boys were tugging at a large roll of wire netting. Nick had found two amongst the piles of rubbish in Copper's paddock. The rolls were badly rusted but he reckoned they could salvage enough to use on Elvis's yards.

The rolls had been half buried, couch grass matted through them. Nick had dug away as much dirt and grass as he could, and they'd extracted one roll without too much struggle. But the second was clinging to the ground.

'Wish we had Jaz,' Matt grumbled.

'Yeah, well, we don't.'

After they brought Elvis home from school that

afternoon, Jaz changed out of her school uniform and headed straight back to town.

'We could do with some help fixing the yards, you know,' Nick had yelled at her as she left the house.

'Get real.'

'He's your horse, too,' Matt added.

She screwed up her face at him. 'Yeah, sure.'

'Come on, Matty.' Nick slapped his little brother on the back, and bent down to tug at the netting again. 'We'll get it this time.'

By the time the boys had pulled the netting free and pushed the two rolls across the paddock to Elvis's pen, their father was arriving home in Turbo. He sat in the car for a while, watching the boys shift one roll into place next to the pen. The colt's head was poking over the side gate, nodding. Ray opened the car door and stepped out.

To the boys' surprise, instead of going into the house, Ray joined them. They stood back from the roll of netting, trying to read their father's mood as he sauntered towards the pen.

'What's this, then?' he asked, tipping his head at the sagging wires and the hole Elvis had dug. The boys told their father what had happened at school. They expected him to scowl.

'He's turning into a real handful, this donkey of yours,' he said to Matt, gazing back at Elvis who was still craning his neck over the gate.

'We're gunna keep him in this time,' Matt tried to assure his father. 'Nick says this'll do it.' He pointed at the rolls of rusty, buckled netting.

'That stuff?' Their father shook his head. Not a hope, he almost said, but then he saw the enthusiasm in Matt's eyes. 'I've got a better idea,' he said instead, and strode towards Turbo.

'Where's he going?' Matt asked. Nick shrugged his shoulders.

'Get yourselves some afternoon tea,' their father called back to them. 'Won't be long.'

The boys had finished their slabs of bread and chocolate spread, and were sitting on the back verandah with a glass of cordial each, when their father returned. Their mother had arrived home and was complaining to them through the kitchen window about the mess they'd left on the table, when Turbo came backing down along the side of the hedge towards Elvis's pen. The lid of the boot was up, and a large roll of silvery netting was poking out.

'What's he up to now?' Mary asked, her voice spiked with exasperation.

'We're fixing Elvis's yards,' Matt said, 'so that he'll never get out.' He drew breath to mention the trouble at school with the colt, but Nick elbowed him in the ribs. The two boys leapt from the verandah and ran down to their father.

'There's way too much netting here for the job,' Ray explained to his sons as he lifted the roll from the car. 'But it was the smallest they had.'

He'd also bought some thin tie-wire to secure the netting, and borrowed a set of wire strainers to tighten the wires that Nick and Matt had strung.

They worked for the rest of the afternoon, and then into evening, using Turbo's one headlight in the dark. They worked quietly, Ray giving instructions from time to time. When Mary called them to eat, he barely raised his head. He told the boys to go, but they stayed.

'Not bad,' their father said when they finally completed the job.

The three of them surveyed the pen in the fading

light of Turbo's headlamp. Their father had straightened the corner posts and rammed the earth around them again with a crowbar. He'd realigned the steel droppers, and strained the plain wires until they were tight. Then they'd attached the new netting, securing it to the top and bottom wires with the tie-wire.

Ray strolled across to Turbo, leaned in the window and turned off the headlight. 'Let's hope we can keep him in this time,' he said from the dark.

Elvis was standing near the clothes line. The lights from the house reflected in his eyes like tiny flames.

Their plates lay on the kitchen table, the food cold. Hungry after their work, the boys and Ray ate quickly. As they were finishing, Mary came to stand in the doorway, her arms folded. The boys looked up from their plates. The man kept eating.

'How much, Ray?' she asked. 'The netting.'

'Not much.' He continued fiddling with his food.

'How much!'

'I dunno,' he mumbled at the table. 'Bit over a hundred. Hundred and sixty.'

'Are you mad?'

'We can use it in other places.'

'On that bloody horse! One hundred and . . . '
Mary snapped her mouth shut.

'We had to, Mary. To keep him in.'

'You know what I'd do with him, don't you!'

'Yeah, I know what you'd do with him.' Ray looked up at his wife. 'But I can't.'

Mary huffed. 'Should be your middle name. Can't do this, can't do that. Can't do any-bloody-thing.'

'You'd know.'

They weren't shouting. They were arguing, but not yelling, their voices tired. Then, like two boxers with no more energy left, they simply stared at each other.

Two lonely headlands, held apart by
the hand of an angry sea.

Mary remained in the doorway for a little longer. 'Jeez!' she eventually hissed through her teeth, and left the room.

Ray didn't say anything. He glanced quickly at his sons, and then stared back at the table top. His hands were trembling, his mouth set tight, and the veins on the side of his head were standing out.

chapter sixteen

Matt lay in bed, wide awake, one hand resting on his island picture book on the blanket beside him. He'd been awake for hours, listening to the colt pacing back and forth. Elvis had stopped whinnying at last, but he still made soft fretting sounds, and Matt knew the foal was staring towards the house. He heard Elvis huff loudly, and start pacing again.

The last three nights had been the same. The days were no different. Every morning, Elvis tried to escape through the gate when Matt came to feed him. He called to the girl, and to the boys, when they left for school. He called to the man. He even called to the woman.

Matt let him out as soon as he got home from school, and took him for long walks in the field across the dirt road. He led the colt with a rope clipped to the halter. But when it was time to enter his pen, Elvis would rear back, pull away and run around the side of the house. The man and the two boys had to herd him down to the back of the garden, waving their arms, forcing him into his pen. It upset the foal, and it upset Matt.

Once they'd shut him in, Matt gave Elvis his milk, even though his mother said that the colt had to be weaned because the powdered milk cost too much. The boy then stood with the foal until it was dark, brushing him and whispering to him, trying to calm him down.

There was never any hurry to go back inside. The family would only sit at the table, eating in stiff silence. Then they would wash the dishes in the same silence. As soon as possible, Nick would hide in his bedroom; Jaz would go to hers, ready to sneak out when she thought it was safe. The parents would sit in front of the television. And Matt would go back outside to wait with Elvis until bedtime.

Matt slid out of bed, collected his shoes and crept from the bedroom. The hallway creaked as he tiptoed down it. The back door squeaked. He stepped across the verandah and down the stairs, hearing the soft call of the colt as he ran through the dewy grass to the yards. Soon he was standing next to Elvis, his head resting against the colt's neck, feeling the thump of his heart and the tremble that ran through his body.

A grumbling far below, deep beneath the island.
A volcano being born. An earthquake waking.

*

The colt stood back from the fence, snorting. The people had gone long ago, and he'd given up calling to them. His nose was bleeding; his chest, too, from where he'd hurled himself at the netting, trying to force his way through. He'd broken the top plain wire where it was rusty, and the netting now sagged. The wound on Elvis's rump had also re-opened, from rubbing it against one of the rough corner posts.

He reared on his hind legs and struck the ground with his front hoofs. He stood for a moment longer, panting. Then he galloped at the fence. He'd already done this several times, baulking at the last minute, swerving to the side or colliding with the fence.

This time he jumped.

He thrust his front legs forward and sprang with his haunches. The run-up was short, and the fence was higher than he'd judged. He cleared it, but only with his front legs. For a moment the colt hung there, balanced in a straddle across the netting. He kicked out with his hind legs, his front hoofs flailing at the air. He tossed his head, wriggled and twisted sideways, and eventually tumbled to the ground on the other side of the fence.

*

The boys saw the police car parked at the front of the house as they walked home along the dirt track. Their mother and father were talking to Sergeant Jenkins near the front gate. Mary had her arms folded. Ray was shuffling his boots in the dirt.

Matt and Nick dropped low at once, slipping through the tangled fence into Copper's paddock and sneaking across to the side gate. Matt looked for Elvis. The colt was not in his pen.

'What's happened?' he said, panic in his voice.

'He must've escaped again,' Nick hissed as they ran, pointing at the buckled netting on the yard.

When they reached the gate, Matt sighed with relief. Elvis was grazing peacefully near the clothes line. Matt ran through the gate, straight to the colt, dropped his school bag and stared at the cut on the young horse's chest, the scratches on his legs, the weeping wound on his rump.

'Elvis,' he whispered to the young horse, gently touching the gash on his chest, burying his head in his mane. 'You idiot!'

Elvis made a soft muffled sound.

Nick stood back and watched his brother. He heard the police car drive away, and the front door slam shut. A moment later, his father appeared at the side of the house. Nick glanced at him, then picked up Matt's bag, trudged up the back steps and disappeared inside.

Ray took a deep breath. 'Your mother was right,' he called out to Matt. 'He's nothing but trouble, this feller.'

Matt looked up and Elvis snorted.

It was a long list of disasters. Elvis had trampled several gardens in the town, and frightened at least one old lady. He'd cracked the front window of the newsagency. He'd kicked a car that had come up behind him in the main street and beeped, bending the grille and breaking one of the headlights. Later, he'd chased some chickens until two had dropped dead. And he'd gone after Marty the postman.

'Poor bloody Marty,' Ray laughed. 'He's got a real thing about dogs chasing him. Bet he didn't know what to do when he saw a horse on his tail.'

He tried to rub the colt's forehead. Elvis pulled back. Ray held out his hand and let the colt sniff it.

'Thing is,' he said after a long pause. 'Sergeant Jenkins says we should get rid of him, by rights.'

Matt stared at his father in disbelief.

'Don't look at me like that! Your mum's furious,' Ray continued. 'She's had enough. We're going to have to pay for the newsagent's window, and for the car. We can't afford that sort of thing, Matty.'

'No, Dad,' Matt begged. 'Please. He just wants to be free.'

'He's an escape artist, mate. Who knows where he'll go next time? He might wander onto the main road and cause a nasty accident. If that happened, we'd have to put him down.'

'Down where?'

'Destroy him,' Ray explained.

Matt threw his arms around the colt's neck. 'I won't let him go, Dad.'

'We don't have much choice,' Ray tried to insist.

'He trusts us!' Matt yelled, his face twisted. 'We can't just throw him away like a bit of rubbish. He's one of us, Dad!'

The man closed his eyes, lowering his head, and pressed at his forehead with his fingers. He knew that his wife and Sergeant Jenkins were right, in their sensible way. But he also knew that Matt was right.

'There is one other thing Sergeant Jenkins said we could try. Elvis won't like it. But it's all we've got left.'

chapter seventeen

'They're awful, Dad. He'll hate them.'

Matt stared at the thick leather straps, screwing up his face. He'd agreed that they would hobble Elvis, but he hadn't really thought it right through, even though his father had explained. The leather straps would be buckled around the colt's front ankles, the short chain between them allowing him to take only very small steps. To hobble.

Sergeant Jenkins had told Ray where he could borrow a pair. Earlier that morning Ray went and collected them. After breakfast Matt waited with Elvis until his father returned, feeding the colt his toast and jam. He heard his mother and Jaz in the kitchen. They stared briefly at him through the window.

'We have to.' His father shook the hobbles. 'It's the only way.'

'He'll go mad,' Matt insisted.

Ray was losing his patience. 'Try to get it into your

head, boy! Either we use these on him, or . . . ' He stopped. Matt was cringing. 'It'll only be for a while,' he continued, his voice softening. 'Until he ... behaves a bit better.'

'Only while I'm at school,' Matt insisted.

'Of course.' Ray rested his hand on Matt's shoulder. 'At least he won't have to stay in the pen all day, if we put these on him. He can wander about, even out the front, if he wants to.'

Matt thought for a moment. 'Just until we get a proper paddock for him, somewhere,' he said. 'So he can run free like a real horse.'

'Yeah, okay,' Ray agreed, pleased to see his son coming round. He held out the hobbles. 'We'd best get this done. You have to be at school, and I should've been at work already.'

The colt stood quietly as Matt held him and Ray strapped the hobbles in place. Even when they stepped back, Elvis did nothing.

But then he tried to move.

His eyes grew wide and round. He shuffled a few steps, stumbling forward, only just regaining his balance. He reared on his hind legs, trying to bite at the leather straps. He fell over, rolled on the ground, kicking, squealing.

Matt stepped towards the colt, but his father grabbed his arm.

'Leave him,' he insisted. 'He has to struggle at first. He has to learn.'

'Learn what?' Matt shouted through his tears. 'That we can't be trusted? That we're cruel?' Matt couldn't take his eyes off the colt. Elvis was writhing and twisting on the ground. He rolled on his back, striking at the air with his hobbled front legs, lashing out with his hind ones.

'I said, leave him!' Ray wrapped his arms around the boy. 'We've got to do this.'

Matt tried to wriggle free, but his father held him tight. He stared down at Elvis as the colt grunted and squealed.

Gradually the colt's kicking and thrashing died down. Then he stopped struggling completely. He lay still, snorting into the grass, staring up at Matt. There was no anger in the eyes, or blame. Only fear and confusion. The boy tried to look away, but he couldn't.

Matt was late for school. He sat silently in the car

as they drove, staring down at the battered picture book in his lap. But all he saw was Elvis's eyes.

'We had to do it, Matty,' Ray said as his son climbed out of the car. Matt closed the door and walked through the school gate without looking back.

*

Ray pushed the broom hard. Any harder and he would have broken the handle. The boss's threats were still jabbing at him.

'If you're late one more time, Turner, you're out.'

Ray tried to explain, about his son and the horse. But the boss wasn't interested.

'One more time!' he snapped, and walked away.

After the morning-tea break, the boss was shouting at him again. Ray hadn't meant to leave the gate open. He'd been spraying down the delivery yard and had forgotten for a minute about the two different mobs of cattle. The whole lot had become mixed up.

'I'll sort them out,' Ray tried to assure the boss.

'Not good enough, Turner,' the boss yelled. 'You either smarten up real fast, or you go! Understood?'

Oh yeah, he understood. He knew exactly what the boss was saying: You're useless, Turner, totally useless. Can't even push a broom without stuffing things up. Can't do this. Can't do that.

Then, at lunchtime, he was sure that the others were staring at him, whispering, laughing. No good, that Turner. Total loser. Can't keep his family together. His wife's got some other bloke on the side. And have you seen his daughter lately? She's wild. And what about that horse they've got, eh? Mad as a meat axe.

Ray bit into his roll, the bread tough and stale, staring blankly across the empty table as he chewed. He swallowed hard, slurping some coffee to wash the dry bread down. He took another bite and threw the roll back into his lunch box.

At least it was almost knock-off time, Ray told himself as he swept. He could go home and . . . and what? He stopped sweeping, and stood glaring at the ground. His elder son was surly. His daughter took no notice of him. His younger son was frightened of him, and now, after the hobbles that morning, resentful as well. And his wife . . . Ray resumed pushing his broom.

He heard the laughter. The slaughtermen were leaving. He saw them appear at the steps above him, smoking, joking. The Green boy was laughing louder than anyone. The young man looked down and his eyes met Ray's. For a moment the laughter stopped, but the man at the bottom of the steps could still hear it.

Laugh at me, will you?

Ray dropped the broom and ran up the steps.

chapter eighteen

Matt didn't wait for Nick after school, but ran home. He'd worried the whole day, wondering how the foal had coped with the hobbles. He sprinted down the dirt path to the side gate. Elvis was standing near the clothes line, as though he hadn't moved all day. His head was down, his back to Matt.

The boy called out, pushed through the gate and strode towards the horse.

'Hey, Elvis!' he yelled.

The colt lifted his head slightly, glanced sideways, then turned away with his ears flattened. Matt stopped, a frown sliding over his face.

'Don't be like that,' he pleaded, reaching towards the colt. 'We're just trying to . . . '

Elvis flicked his tail and hopped away a few paces.

Matt sighed, his arm dropping. 'Okay, then,' he said. 'Have it your way.'

He waited, hoping the foal might turn and hobble

towards him. But Elvis remained sullenly still. Matt shrugged and ambled to the back steps.

On the verandah, he paused and turned around. 'Two can play that game, you know,' he said. Then he went inside.

Matt made himself a glass of chocolate milk and two pieces of bread with butter and honey. He spread plenty of butter, covering it with a thick layer of creamed honey. As he bit into the first slice, he peeped out the kitchen window. He saw Elvis lift his head and look around. Matt smiled to himself, and tapped at the window. The colt pricked his ears and peered towards the house. The boy took another bite, sipped his milk, then went back outside and sat on the top step.

As soon as the boy appeared, the colt flattened his ears and turned his head away. Matt ignored him, slurping loudly at his milk, munching on his bread. Eventually, Elvis turned his head back. Then, slowly, his body. With short, intermittent hops, he gradually brought his front half around until he was facing Matt.

The boy continued eating and drinking, not letting himself look up. But he noticed Elvis moving. From the corner of his eye he saw the foal edging slowly towards him. Matt sat still, even though he was bursting inside with excitement. He wanted to leap up, run to Elvis and hug him. But he buried his face in his glass of milk and waited. Let him come to you, he told himself. Eventually the colt was standing at the bottom of the steps.

He stretched his head up towards the boy. Matt put down his glass and grinned. Then he slid down the steps, and rubbed the bony bit on the front of Elvis's forehead, scratched it hard with his fingers. The horse pushed closer. Matt put his head next to Elvis's, and they rubbed their foreheads together, the colt's big lashes blinking close to the boy's eyes.

'I thought I'd lost you,' Matt whispered. Elvis nickered. 'But I just had to wait, didn't I?'

Matt looked down at his hand. The honey was dripping through his fingers. He gave the colt the rest of his bread, then leant down and unbuckled the hobbles. Elvis chewed on the bread and snuffled for more. Matt let the foal lick his fingers.

'Come on.'

He leapt up and strode along the side of the house, through the front gate, and across the gravel road into the big field. Elvis followed. Matt stopped and lay his arm across Elvis's withers.

'Well?' he laughed. 'What are you waiting for?' He lifted his arm and lightly slapped the colt on the rump.

Elvis took off. He galloped right round the field a couple of times, jumping logs, kicking and calling out. But all the while he kept his eye on the boy, looking back to check that he was still there. If Matt turned around and walked away, the colt galloped up behind him, and followed like a shadow. As soon as Matt had rubbed and scratched him, he ran off again.

The boy and the young horse moved further and further from the house. When the colt had galloped and kicked enough, he joined the boy and ambled beside him. They explored. Rabbit holes, dead logs, birds. Elvis inspected a huge nest of ants too closely, and the insects swarmed over his muzzle. He galloped off, snorting and coughing and rubbing his nose on the ground.

When Matt looked back towards the house, all he could see was the roof, a tiny mound of brown tin, dwarfed by the mountains behind. Over these, a bank of dark clouds gathered.

We swam right out into the bay, to the edge of the reef. We let the sun soak into us, not worried about sharks or sea monsters, or the waves swelling on the reef. We barely noticed the storm brewing out to sea. And we thought nothing of the rumbling under the island. We were swimming together.

*

It was nearly dark when Matt and Elvis arrived home. They heard the arguing before they reached the gate.

The mountains growled and the ground trembled.

Matt's mother was shouting, her voice sharp and jagged. Jaz was too. An occasional mumble came from his father.

'You can't even push a broom!' Mary's voice shrieked through the walls.

'You don't know what it's like,' the man muttered. 'The way they . . . '

'Don't give me that crap! You're useless, that's what you are!'

Matt sneaked along the side of the house, Elvis behind him. He tried not to listen, pressed his hands over his ears. But the angry words cut through his fingers.

The wind scowled at the sea, whipping it wild.
Waves reared up, their manes blown back,
then lunged forward, smashing themselves
against ragged cliffs.

Nick was sitting on the back steps, hunched over his up-drawn knees, his arms wrapped around his legs. He was crying, his arched body shuddering. Matt felt his chest tighten, and he clenched his fists.

'I've had it!' the mother's words tore through the walls. 'You and this stinking, rotten life!'

Nick straightened when he saw his brother approaching, quickly wiping his face with his sleeve and blowing his nose.

Matt sat down next to him. Elvis stood a few paces back and watched the boys.

'Mum's leaving,' Nick said after a while.

'How do you know?'

'You deaf?'

Matt flinched at his brother's anger, and then at the screech of his mother's voice. 'You won't work, that's your problem! You just want to hang about the house and do nothing all day!'

'Someone's got to be at home,' Matt's father's voice was louder now. 'For the kids.'

'Don't make me laugh. You couldn't give a stuff about the kids!'

'Dad lost his job at the abattoir,' Nick continued. 'He tried to bash up Jaz's boyfriend.'

'Why?'

'I dunno! Why's he do anything?' Nick gave a long sigh and shook his head. 'Anyway, Mum's going.'

He spat on the ground.

'Where?' Matt asked.

'Friend's place.'

'Where's that?'

'Jeez, Matt! What's it matter where he lives?'

'He?'

'Yeah, he! Mum's goin' off to live with another man. Happens all the time with people like us!' Nick spat again, and then noticed that his little brother was trembling. 'Somewhere in Grayston.'

*The mountains stamped, the earth shuddered,
and the ground split apart. A crack opened wide,
like a hungry mouth. Get away!*

'Jaz is goin' too,' Nick added
'With Mum?'
'S'pose so. Dunno. Don't care.'

The colt stepped closer to the boys, his ears flickering at the shouts from the house. Matt reached out and rubbed the foal on his forehead, trying to block out the racket.

'It's always me who has to work. You've never stuck at a job!' A door slammed. Then another.

'What about us?' Matt asked.

'What about us?'

'Who are we gunna go with?'

Nick didn't reply. He simply stared at the ground.

Elvis pushed his muzzle into Matt's hand, nibbling at it with his soft lips. Matt breathed in the colt's familiar horsey smell, as the shouting swirled around them.

Get away!

'Why don't we go too?' Matt said. 'Run away.'

Nick shook his head and huffed.

'Why not?' Matt continued, his eyes wide. 'You and me.'

'And that silly horse of yours, too, I suppose?'

'He's not silly! Elvis'll be a great horse one day.'

Nick laughed and looked away. 'Yeah, sure. In your dreams.'

Matt jumped to his feet. 'You're just like them,' he shouted. 'You only know how to hurt.' Matt rushed to the colt's side and threw his arm around his neck, glaring down at Nick. 'Elvis would never do that!'

Both boys heard the front door slam and their father shout from inside the house. Matt pulled his arm away from the foal, struck at the air with both fists, then spun around and ran.

Run, run! Down to the beach. Into the water.
Away from the island, the rumbling,
juddering, crumbling island.

'Matty!'

Matt didn't stop. He ran down through the garden

to the back gate. Elvis turned and stared intently, his ears straight up. Then he squealed and galloped after the boy. Nick heard Turbo start, rev a few times, then drive away.

'Don't be stupid! Matty!'

Matt stumbled against the gate, Elvis behind him, nudging at the boy with his head, making sharp, fretful squeaks. Matt clawed at the latch, ripping it back, thrust the gate open and lurched into the dark.

Out into the deep, fins all around. Screams swallowed by the snapping and the thrashing, waves crashing on the rocks. Get away! Swim hard. Save yourself. Get away!

He saw Turbo's headlight flicker through the trees, like a lighthouse beam, as the car sped along the gravel track. He ran down to the creek near the main road, Elvis at his side. He stopped for a moment, panting, sobbing. The colt sniffed at the thin trickle of water.

Matt heard the roar of Turbo on the main road as he staggered along the creek and across it. He scrambled up the bank and saw the tail lights slipping away into the night like little flames. He yelled out. The flames flickered, and then were gone. He stood in the dark with the colt.

'Matty!'

Nick ran to the gate. He called again. There was no reply. He glanced up at the house, wondering if he should sprint back and get his father.

'What's the point?' he muttered angrily, then stepped through the gate and strode towards the creek.

chapter nineteen

'Matty!'

What have I done? Ray stood at the side of the road, squinting ahead into the dark, his mind seething with uncertainty. He'd walked for over half an hour, searching, calling. But there was no sign of the boy or the foal. Perhaps they went the other way, towards Hillview. Ray glanced over his shoulder. No. Nick said he was sure. But then, Nick could have made a mistake in the dark.

Ray cupped his hands to his mouth and called as loud as he could. 'Matty!'

After his wife and daughter had driven off in Turbo, Ray waited in the sitting room, staring blankly at its emptiness. Then he stepped into the hall, flinching at its silence. He knew his sons were outside, on the verandah, or hiding in the dark with the horse. He knew he should go and find them. And say something. But what?

What do you say to your kids when you're useless? Why would they listen to a loser? He fumbled in his pockets, pulled out his cigarettes. His hands shook as he lit one. He walked towards the front door, drawing in the smoke, opened the door and stepped outside.

He had no idea how long he'd wandered in the dark, down the gravel road, the night wrapped around him like a cloak, the grey trees bending over him. Ray couldn't get the voices out of his head, and the faces. His wife sneering at him, Jaz in tears.

'How could you, Dad? Craig never hurt you. Why did you hit him?'

Ray didn't have an answer. Except that he was useless, good for nothing.

He stopped next to a tree. In his mind, Jaz's perplexed face was staring at him. Then she ran from the sitting room, crying. His wife followed. Doors slammed. Turbo drove away. And the stark reality slapped him in the face.

Ray leant against the tree, staring down the gravel road, hoping he might see Turbo returning. He clenched his fist, pressing it against his mouth, biting it as he fought back his own tears. He smashed his fist against the tree. It hurt as his knuckles thudded against the hard trunk. He winced, then punched again, slamming into the tree with both fists until the pain numbed in his hands. Then he pressed his forehead against the tree and cried.

'Dad!' Nick was running down the road towards him. 'I've been looking everywhere for you.' He panted, struggling to catch his breath. 'Matty's gone!'

'What do you mean?'

'He just took off. With Elvis. Up the road.'

'Which way?' his father asked.

'Grayston.'

'You sure?'

'Pretty sure,' Nick gasped.

Ray rushed back to the house with Nick, leaving the boy at home in case Mary and Jaz returned while he was out searching for Matt.

'I won't be long,' he told his older son, reaching towards him. 'I'm sorry . . . ' he began.

Nick pulled back, staring at his father's bleeding fists.

Ray didn't finish what he'd wanted to say.

*

'Where are you, Matty?'

Ray's voice was husky from calling. The white posts at the side of the road ticked past like long minutes. An owl hooted overhead, a fox ran across his path. Cars loomed up at him, slowing suspiciously before accelerating past.

The lights of a car approached from the direction of Grayston. Ray stepped into the middle of the road, waving his arms. The car stopped.

'A boy,' he shouted in at the car window. 'A little boy and a horse. Seen them?'

'Yeah,' the face in the car replied. 'Just over the hill.'

Ray ran.

'Matty!'

Matt stopped and looked back, thinking that he'd heard his name. Just a noise, he decided. A dog barking somewhere, a distant car, probably just his imagination. The night was full of noises. He heard an owl hoot in the distance, and glanced nervously around at the eerie night.

*Treading water in a coal black sea. The dread
of all alone. The cold unknown. How long
before the tentacles drag you down?*

Cars seemed to pounce out of the dark as they came hurtling around corners, blinding Matt with their harsh lights. A few beeped their horns, scaring Elvis as they shot past, making him shy sideways. One almost hit the colt. Matt kept to the rough ground away from the bitumen, struggling through the thick, high grass, stumbling in holes, tripping over logs and sticks that hid in the darkness. His legs were tired and his feet ached.

Eventually he stopped, exhausted. The road dipped into a gully and crossed a small bridge. There was a stream running under the bridge. Elvis drank from it, and then nudged at Matt. The boy slumped to the ground.

'Matty!'

The voice was real. Matt sat up. He heard his name again. He yelled back as loud as he could.

'Dad! Down here!'

Ray hugged Matt until the boy winced. 'I'm sorry,'

he repeated over and over, his voice trembling. 'I'll make things better. I promise.'

They didn't go home straight away, but stayed sitting beside the stream, Matt with his head on his father's lap, Elvis grazing nearby. Matt listened to the whispers of the water, the soft munching of Elvis, and felt the warm roughness of his father's hand stroking his brow, the darkness folding around them like a blanket.

Our raft creaked and groaned, and lay low in the water with the weight of us. The sea lapped over the edge, and we had to lie very still so that it wouldn't tip. But I felt safe.

'Matty?'

The boy was asleep. Ray sat for a while longer, gazing at the grazing horse. Then he stood, lifting Matt into his arms. The boy made a small noise, but stayed asleep.

'Come on, Elvis,' the man whispered. 'We've got a long way to go.' He turned and clambered back up to the road. The colt followed.

chapter twenty

Nick grimaced. 'Not sausages again?'

'Looks like it,' Ray replied. He placed the plates of cheap sausages and instant mashed potato in front of his boys. 'We've got a choice of sauces, but,' he added with a weak grin, pointing to the three different bottles.

Nick made patterns with his fork in his potato.

'I like sausages,' Matt said.

He and his father had spent the afternoon with Elvis. Ray had washed Elvis's halter, and the colt looked very smart as he pranced along. They'd walked into town, leading the colt. Then they'd circled back around the outskirts of Werrawee, through the countryside. Matt showed his father how he could sit on Elvis's back, hanging onto his mane as the colt trotted along. Then they let the colt gallop and explore.

'Yeah, but not every night,' Nick replied, stabbing a sausage with his fork.

'We'll have pizza tomorrow,' his father said. 'I've

got some work down at the hardware store for the next few days, so we can live it up.' Ray tried not to make too much of the work. 'Out the back, packing and lifting things. Only on trial, but who knows?'

'We might get pizza every night, Nick,' Matt said. Nick nodded half-heartedly.

It was five days since Jaz and Mary had left. The house seemed filled with their absence. No Jaz hogging the bathroom in the morning. No early morning sounds of their mother making breakfast, no music from Jaz's room, no tell-tale creak anymore as she climbed out her window and sneaked along the verandah at night. No rock-and-rolling with Mum.

But the boys felt the absence most when they sat down to eat. Where there had once been five of them crowding around the table, now there were only three. Matt still expected his mother and sister to walk through the door at any moment, as though they'd just been watching television. But each night only their chairs were at the table.

'I know this is hard,' Ray said as Nick continued prodding the sausage. 'But it's all a bit new to me, see.'

Nick kept his face down. Matt leaned over,

speared his fork into one of Nick's unwanted sausages and began munching it straight off the fork. 'I'll have a look at one of Mum's cookbooks, if you like. See if I can knock up something a bit better next time, eh? Or maybe you could, Nick. You're good with books.'

Nick gave a brief nod, but still didn't look up.

'It's okay, Dad,' Matt mumbled through a mouthful. 'This'll just make us really like Mum's food when she comes back.'

Nick and his father both stared at Matt.

He stopped chewing and stared back. 'What?'

'She's not coming back,' Nick replied, letting his fork clatter onto the plate.

The father frowned at his older son. 'Nick!'

'Well, she isn't.' Nick stood up, pushing back his chair .

'She might.' Matt glared at his brother, swallowing his mouthful with difficulty. 'You don't know everything.'

'Whatever,' Nick mumbled and left the table.

Ray sat grinding his teeth as Nick slouched into the kitchen with his plate.

'Doesn't Mum love us any more?' Matt asked his

father. 'Only Jaz. Is that why she took her and left us?'

Ray reached across the table and rested his hand on Matt's arm. 'Of course she loves you. She loves you and Nick more than anything, mate.'

'And you too, Dad.'

Ray didn't reply. He stood up and began clearing the bowls from the table. Matt picked up the plates and followed him into the kitchen, where Nick was staring silently into the sink.

Ray leaned awkwardly around Nick, placing the bowls in the sink. Nick edged away slightly. Matt handed the plates to his father, a knife sliding off and rattling across the kitchen floor. Nick frowned. Matt picked up the knife and handed it to his father. Ray placed it quietly on the sink, and then the three of them stood in tense silence.

Ray opened his arms. Matt leant into him at once, letting himself be pulled against his father's side. Nick held back for a moment, scowling at the floor. Then he too allowed himself to become part of the bundle.

Three on the leaky raft drifting in the sea,
wishing there were five.

chapter twenty-one

Ray got up early and cleaned the house. Breakfast was on the table, and the boys' lunch was ready. Sandwiches, captured tight in clingy plastic.

'Right. Things are going to be different from now on.' Ray greeted his sons at the breakfast table. 'I've thought about this all night.'

He looked so fresh and clean. He had shaved, for a start. Ray never shaved in the morning. Hardly ever shaved, full stop. Mary used to say his face was like a toilet brush. He'd washed his hair too, was wearing clean clothes, and smelt of soap.

'There's sausage sandwiches with sauce for you, Matt.' Ray handed the package over. 'And the same with barbecue sauce for you, Nicko.' He grinned as he held up his older son's sandwiches. 'Just kidding, mate. Peanut butter okay?' He threw the sandwiches to Nick. 'Anyone for more toast?'

The boys stared at him.

'What are you two gawking at?'

'You look different, Dad,' Nick said.

'Got to make a good impression at the store. If all goes well, I might even get more days.'

Ray munched quickly into his toast and slurped his coffee. Then he grinned at the boys and rubbed his hands together. 'Like I said, things are going to be different. We've got to pull ourselves up, you know what I mean? Out of this hole. Get a life!'

The boys glanced at each other.

'That's it. Get a life. Starting today.' Ray stood up and began clearing the breakfast things. 'It means we're all going to have to pull our weight. You're in charge of the shopping, Nick, and the cooking. Reckon you're up to it?'

Nick bobbed his head up and down. 'No more sausages!' he said. 'Great!'

'But I like sausages,' Matt whined.

'Maybe once a week, then,' Nick said.

'And we'll keep the house super clean and tidy,' the father shouted from the sink. 'You guys look after your bedrooms and, let's say, the sitting room. I'll do the kitchen and bathroom. How's that sound?'

'What about the verandah?' Nick asked.

'Good one. This weekend we'll clean that verandah like never before. Get rid of the boxes and rubbish, chuck out the table and those dirty old armchairs, and give the whole verandah a big wash.'

'But Guts and TriHard,' Matt said. 'Where will they live?'

'We'll give them a wash too!' Ray replied. 'They won't know what hit them.'

'They'll freak!' Nick laughed. 'They've never been washed.'

'Yeah,' Matt shouted. 'We'll make everything clean and new again. We'll get it all so clean that if . . . when Mum and Jaz come back, they'll want to stay for ever and ever!'

'That's right, Matty,' his father said, with a warning glance at Nick.

'What about Elvis?' Nick asked.

'We'll wash him too,' Matt replied.

'I tell you what we *will* do,' his father said. 'We'll find out about horses, so we can bring him up proper. I'll ask a few fellers who know about horses, and you might look for some books in the library at school,

Nick. Maybe the librarian can order something in. Training young horses, you know the sort of stuff. We might be able to rent a good paddock somewhere for him too, with good fencing and water, somewhere he can run around and let off steam like a real horse.'

'Then we won't have to hobble him any more,' Matt said. 'We'll throw those horrible hobbles in the garbage bin.'

*

Matt strapped Elvis's hobbles on before he left for school. The colt stamped his feet, reared back and bit at the boy as he tried to do up the buckles. Matt slapped him on the side, and Elvis stood still. But when the boy stood up, the colt's ears were flat against his head.

'Just you wait,' Matt said to the foal. 'There's a big surprise waiting for you.'

The colt watched Matt shoulder his school bag and wander off with the bigger boy. Then the man appeared on the verandah and came down the steps with an apple in his hand, cut into several pieces. He gave them to the colt, waiting with him while he ate. Then he, too, walked out the gate and down the track.

Once all the people had gone, Elvis shuffled around to the shade at the front of the house and stayed there most of the morning, grazing lightly, hobbling from one patch of grass to another.

In the afternoon he watched and listened for signs of the boy's return. He pricked his ears at every noise, at the traffic sliding by on the main road, the sounds drifting in from the town, the plovers in the field, the breeze.

The dusty white truck came along the dirt track from the main road. It paused at the front of the house, idling for a while, then pulled a little way past the house and reversed down beside the post-and-rail fence towards Elvis's pen. The colt watched it through the privet. Two men got out and poked their heads over the side gate. Then they came through the gate, leaving it open, and walked towards Elvis. He shuffled away, but they kept coming.

chapter twenty-two

'Thank you, Michael, for sharing that news. Does anyone else have news for this afternoon?'

Miss Barnet looked around the class. Matt kept his head down. He had news, all right. It was bursting inside him. He wanted to shout it out, but he wasn't game enough.

The class had laughed at his island book. They'd laughed the first time he told them about Copper. And again when he'd talked about the yards he and Nick built for Elvis. They laughed every time Elvis escaped —when he broke the newsagent's window, when he chased Marty the postman, and especially when he destroyed the school's horticultural patch. Matt didn't want to be laughed at any more.

'Matt?' Miss Barnet was smiling across at him. 'We haven't heard about Elvis for a while.'

Matt shifted uneasily in his seat.

'He must be lots of fun now.'

'Yes, Miss.' Matt still held back.

'He must be growing. I bet he's becoming quite a handful.'

'Yes, Miss, he is. We've had a bit of trouble with him, you know.' The class burst out laughing. Matt flinched, but kept going when Miss Barnet smiled at him. He stood up and raised his voice. 'He's getting better, but.' The laughter died down.

'So what are you doing with him now?' Miss Barnet asked.

'We hobble him in the day so's he can't escape. After school I take the hobbles off and we go exploring.' Matt told the class about how fast Elvis could gallop, and how high he could jump. 'I can ride him too, bareback.'

'So when will you put a saddle on him?'

'Not sure. Me and Nick and Dad don't know much about horses. Hardly nothing. But we're gunna learn. That's what Dad says.' Matt was feeling more excited now, and talked faster. 'Dad's gunna ask someone how you look after horses proper, and Nick's getting some books. And we're gunna find a paddock for Elvis where he can grow up like a real horse.'

Matt took a deep breath. 'That'll be good,' he went on, 'because then when Elvis is better, and we've cleaned up the house and washed the verandah, and the dogs, and got all the rubbish out of the garden, mown the lawn and cut the hedge, Mum and Jaz will come back.'

The classroom was silent.

'Well!' Miss Barnet cleared her throat and clapped her hands together. 'That's wonderful, Matt.' She stepped across to her desk and reached into the drawer. 'I think that was the best news I've ever heard.'

*

The ropes were tight.

One pulled against his neck, cutting off the air until he could barely breathe. Another was lashed behind his rump, and every time he tried to pull back it tightened even more. Several times he reared up, striking at the men. But the ropes pulled him down again. Closer and closer to the dusty white truck.

Onto the ramp. He tugged backwards, throwing his head from side to side, his eyes wide and white with fear. Onto the ramp again, up the ramp, twisted in the shouting, growling tangle of ropes.

Where was the boy?

*

Matt was still smiling to himself as he left school. He'd tell Dad and Nick, and Mum and Jaz when he saw them. He'd tell Elvis too. The teacher had given him not one golden sticker, not two, but three.

Then Matt saw Simon Croft and his mates outside the school gate, and his smile disappeared. They were waiting for their bus. No Nick in sight—he was at sport. Matt tried to hurry past, head down. But Simon stood in the way.

Matt stopped. He didn't want any trouble, especially from Simon Croft. The boy was bigger than him.

'What do you want?' Matt asked.

'Dad has seen that colt of yours.'

'So?'

Simon shuffled his shoes. 'He says it's a good type.'

Matt wondered whether he'd heard properly.

'Dad says he knew the old mare too, and that she

was a top horse once, and that Elvis could be also.'

'Yeah?' Suddenly Matt was more interested.

'As long as he's looked after proper, that is. Dad says Elvis could turn into a rotten horse if he's not handled well. He reckons he could do a really good job on Elvis.'

Matt was suspicious again. He wasn't about to let anyone get their hands on Elvis. 'Once we get a paddock we'll do a good job on him, too. Me and Nick and Dad.'

'We've got a spare paddock,' Simon said. 'I could ask Dad, if you want.'

Matt didn't know what to think. Simon was the smart kid in the class, who lived on a big farm and knew everything about horses. Why was he saying this? There had to be a catch.

'I've got Gonzo, see. About the same age as Elvis. And Dad likes to work a couple of horses at a time.'

Matt looked at Simon and his mates carefully, searching for any sign of tricks. A smirk, or a grin from one of the boys.

'Anyway, ask your dad if you want.'

'Okay.' Matt edged past the group of boys and

walked off. After he'd gone a few paces, he turned around to see if they were snickering behind his back. They weren't. They were just standing there, watching him.

Matt ran home.

*

Elvis was always waiting, and he always called to Matt as soon as he saw the boy. He called this time, too. But the call was different.

It was a call of fear. Matt saw the dusty white truck near the side of the house, and the two men climbing into it. He saw Elvis's muzzle poking through the slats on the side of the truck.

Matt screamed.

He dropped his bag and sprinted down the track as fast as he could. The men saw him. They slammed their doors shut. Elvis cried out, but the revving of the truck was louder. Matt yelled, but the truck was already on the dirt track, rattling past the house, leaving a cloud of dust and diesel fumes.

Matt kept running into the dust, shouting and

yelling. Down the dirt track until his chest ached and his legs grew weak. He fell to his knees, panting. The rev and rattle of the truck faded, the dust drifted across the field, but the cry of the colt stayed in Matt's head.

Born of an earthquake growling leagues below—
tsunami, monster wave. It destroys and devours
all that cowers in its path, washing over islands,
sweeping people out to sea.

chapter twenty-three

'We need you.'

Ray was on the telephone, talking to his wife. Through the kitchen window he could see Matt on the back steps. The boy was hunched into a tiny bundle. He had his island book with him, and was clutching it to his chest. He had calmed down somewhat, though he was still crying, his body shuddering from time to time.

Ray had found the school bag on the track when he walked home from work that afternoon. He discovered Matt further along, lying on the gravel road, sobbing. Ray had to hold his son tight and stroke him gently for a long time before Matt could even begin to tell him what had happened.

'It's Matty,' Ray explained to his wife. 'The horse has been stolen. He's taking it bad, Mary. Bloody bad. He blames himself. And me, too, probably. Friggin' hobbles!'

Ray realised that his hands were shaking. 'He's a

mess. We can't pull him out of it.' He glanced across at his elder son who was sitting up at the kitchen table, listening intently to his father. 'I thought maybe you might . . . ' Ray shrugged his shoulders at Nick. 'Good on ya, luv.'

Ray sighed with relief as he hung up the telephone. 'She's coming,' he told Nick, who smiled and eased back in his chair. Ray peered through the kitchen window at his younger son again. Matt had his knees pressed against his body, his head buried. He was rocking back and forth.

No more raft. Only bits and pieces, scattered
by the wave, devoured by the reef. And after that?
Waiting scared in the water. Then the slow
sinking, as the sea begins to suck you down.

'Made you some chokky milk, mate.'

Matt kept rocking.

'I'll just put it down here, eh?' His father placed the glass on the verandah boards, but kept his hand on the boy's shoulder. 'Mum and Jaz are coming,' he said. 'Shouldn't be too long.'

He could feel his son's body trembling. 'We'll work out what to do. Matty. We'll get him back.' He lifted his hand and clenched it into a fist. 'I promise.'

Ray stood. Nick was at the back door. Their eyes met for a moment, and then the boy left the door and joined his father at Matt's side. The three of them waited on the back steps.

They heard Turbo coming long before it reached the house. Ray recognised the faulty muffler as the car drove along the main road from Grayston, and saw its single headlight winking through the trees. It turned into the gravel road, and a few moments later pulled up at the front gate. Ray and Nick went to meet Mary.

'Where is he?'

Mary was in the house, and then at the back door. Matt wanted to jump up and run to her, but his body was so hunched into itself that he couldn't move. He heard her walk across the verandah and sit beside him. Then his mother's arms wrapped around him.

Matt saw Jaz's sneakers and the legs of her jeans, and then the rest of her when she knelt down. He could see Nick and his father standing back. They were all there together. All except Elvis.

He closed his eyes and pressed his head into his mothers arms.

'They took him, Mum,' he whispered.

Mary felt her son clinging to her, but didn't know what to say. She'd heard the urgency in her husband's voice on the phone, and she knew how deeply Matt was attached to the horse. But none of that had prepared her for the trembling bundle in her arms.

On the way over, she and Jaz had allowed themselves to agree that the loss of Elvis might not be such a bad thing. Now she wasn't so sure.

She squeezed her son tight, and sighed.

*

The family was in the sitting room, Ray in one armchair, his wife in the other with Matt tucked tightly in beside her. Mary was holding the book Matt had been clutching on the verandah. She glanced at it briefly, then placed it on the coffee table.

Nick and Jaz were perched at either end of the lounge.

Mary couldn't help noticing how neat and tidy the room was. The whole house, in fact. Her husband, too.

No stubble, washed hair, clean clothes.

'Looks like you lot don't need me,' she commented, flicking her eyes around the room and finally letting them rest on her husband.

'We do, Mary,' he said holding her gaze.

She huffed and looked away. 'Well then,' she said. 'What now?'

'We get Elvis back,' Ray said simply.

'Do we?' Mary felt Matt tense at her side, and regretted the hardness behind her question.

It was Nick who replied, with a quiet firmness. 'Yes, Mum,' he said. 'We get him back.'

The mother glanced at her daughter to see what her response might be. Jaz was staring at the carpet, fiddling with a loose thread on the arm of the lounge. The girl had been in two minds about coming at all that night. She wanted to see her brothers. She wanted to see her room, too. Jaz had always liked her room. But she wasn't so sure about her father.

'I promised,' Ray said to his wife.

Mary raised her eyebrows, showing her husband what she thought of his promises.

'We have to, Mary.' Ray nodded towards Matt,

lowering his voice. 'Look at him. That horse has come to mean the earth to Matty.'

'It's still just a horse,' Mary whispered. Matt's breathing was slow and regular. She looked down at him and then continued. 'Couldn't we . . . ?'

'You're wrong,' Ray interrupted his wife. 'I can't explain it properly, but that colt is like a . . . lifeline for Matty.' Ray paused for a moment, swallowing hard, appealing to Mary with his eyes, and then to Jaz. 'I know you both think it's crazy, and I don't expect you to help. But it would be so good if you did.'

Mary felt Matty press against her and murmur. She glanced across at her daughter, rolled her eyes and gave a small shrug. Jaz nodded back.

'Better get me a cup of tea, then,' she said.

Floating. But where am I floating? On the water? Under it? Within it. Buoyed yet bound by the fingers of the sea, drifting towards the beach. Hovering weightless near the shore.

'It's someone local,' Mary insisted as she sipped her tea. 'I'm sure I've seen a truck like that around.'

'Why don't we ask Sergeant Jenkins?' Nick suggested.

Ray was not so keen on that idea. Elvis wasn't really their horse, strictly speaking. Besides, he suspected that the sergeant would be pleased to have Elvis out of the way after the trouble he'd caused.

'We should offer a reward,' Nick said.

'Aw yeah,' his mother scoffed. 'Ten thousand do?'

'What about an ad in the newspaper, then?' Nick suggested.

'And who's paying for that?' his mother asked.

'Me,' Ray replied at once. 'I'll pay.'

'We could put up notices at school and in town,' Nick said.

'Maybe at your new school, Jaz?' Ray added. 'Someone in Grayston might have seen something.'

Jaz nodded, but didn't look at her father. 'How are we going to bring Elvis back anyway,' she asked, 'if we do find him? What will we put him in?'

'Good point,' Ray agreed. 'We need a truck. Or a horse trailer.' Jaz shrugged and looked away.

Sometimes Matt could hear the voices clearly. Other times he could only catch the feelings behind the words. And then the voices would fade completely, until he couldn't hear them at all, slipping into a dream: Elvis calling, the rattle of the truck, running through diesel fumes and dust.

'I'd better be going.'

It was late.

Mary looked down at her younger son curled in the crook of her arm. She didn't really want to leave him. The other two dozed on the lounge.

'Stay if you want,' her husband said.

Mary didn't reply. They both sat in silence.

'It's been a lousy day,' Ray said eventually.

'I can see that. You look tired.'

'I just want to get Elvis back, Mary. Neither of us understands what that horse means to Matty. I've watched them together, and it's almost as though they're one, they're that close. Matt has something really special here, and I don't want to let it fade away just because we couldn't be bothered.'

Mary sighed.

She was tired too. 'I know what you mean.'

She extracted herself from the armchair.

'Let's get him to bed.'

chapter twenty-four

*Washed up on the shore, sun dazed, skin crisp
with salt. Seagulls overhead. The rhythmic thwack
of waves, the whoosh as they shimmer up the
beach. Then their soft retreat into silence,
before it all starts again.*

Matt lay in bed, his eyes half open, a shaft of morning sun on his face. He gazed sleepily across the room at the back of Nick's head, hearing magpies outside, a truck changing gears on the Grayston road, someone in the kitchen.

He closed his eyes and breathed in the scent of his mother's perfume that still lingered on the pillow. It was like a dream, one he wished would never end. She had come back! She had put him to bed and lain with him until he fell asleep. But then the dream ended. Matt recalled the growl of Turbo driving off in the night, and it all came flooding back.

Elvis!

He sat up and listened. No neighing from the pen, no clump of hoofs or muffled calls. The truck and the dust had been real. Not a dream. Not even a nightmare.

Matt lay back, squeezed his eyes shut and pulled the blanket over his head.

*

'They're coming over tonight,' Ray assured his son at breakfast. Matt brightened; he stopped prodding his cereal and ate a spoonful.

Even though he knew they'd left in the night, Matt still half expected to see Jaz and his Mum at the breakfast table. He still half expected to see Elvis from the kitchen window. But all he saw was the canister of powdered milk in the cupboard near the breakfast cereal, and the green wine bottle they had used for feeding the foal, the black teat lying next to it on the kitchen window sill.

'Mum said they'll stay for a while,' Nick added. 'Until we sort this out.'

Matt made himself smile and finish his cereal.

Nick held tightly to his brother's hand as they walked away from the house. Matt didn't want to go to school, but his father insisted. He kept looking back. No colt. No call.

In class, he huddled over his desk, wishing the day would end. The laughter of the other kids jangled in his head, along with the teacher's voice, the scraping of chairs and tables, the thump of running in the playground, the shouts of fun.

At lunchtime, Matt sat by himself in a corner of the playground, hoping that no-one would come near. A few kids looked in his direction, but they stayed away.

He closed his eyes and tried to imagine Elvis. He saw him in a field, galloping, his coat shining like red gold. The blaze on his forehead was a silver sword.

'I heard about Elvis.'

Matt glanced up, startled. Simon Croft was standing in front of him. 'How did it happen?'

Matt told Simon about the truck, and how he'd run after it.

'What'll you do?' Simon asked.

'Dunno,' Matt replied. 'We don't even know where he is.'

'My dad might be able to help,' Simon said. 'He might know something. I'll ask him.'

*

Simon's father came to the Turner house that night. Ray gave him a beer and they talked in the sitting room. Matt and Nick sat on the lounge and listened.

'It's Frank Barnes and his son,' James Croft assured them. 'They've got a white truck. They live about ten kilometres out on the Grayston road. He's a nasty piece of work, Frank is. I wouldn't put anything past him.'

'But why?' Ray Turner asked.

'Simple. You know that old mare you had here? She belonged to him. Well, that's what he reckoned anyway. Rumour was he'd stolen her from up north, and he probably did. He worked her hard, treated her bad, and then dumped her in that paddock next to you when she was no good to him any more. That's the sort of bastard he is.'

'So Elvis is really his,' Matt said. The thought worried him.

'No way! He dumped that mare and left her to die. Obviously didn't know she was in foal or he might've looked after her. I bet he didn't come near her once.'

'No,' Ray said. 'Matt and Nick looked after her.'

'So I wouldn't worry too much about Frank Barnes,' Mr Croft winked at Matt. 'He's got no right to that colt of yours. He just happens to know a good horse when he sees one.'

'So how do we make him give Elvis back?' Matt asked.

'You won't. The only way you'll ever get your colt back is to go and steal him yourself.'

Ray and his two sons gaped at the other man. James Croft stared back.

'Fair enough,' Matt's father said at last.

'That's the spirit,' James Croft laughed. 'And if you do get your colt back, give me a call. I've got a spare paddock that would suit him down to the ground. Won't cost you anything. I wouldn't mind handling him a bit. You've got a top one there, if you want my opinion.'

After that, the two men talked for a while outside before James Croft left. Matt and Nick stayed in the sitting room.

'We'll have to do it at night,' Nick said.

Matt nodded, his eyes wide. 'Yeah. Really late.'

'We'll sneak out to the Barnes's farm and . . . '

' . . . and grab Elvis while they're asleep.'

'But how will we get him back home?'

Matt thought for a moment. 'I'll ride him!'

Their father was standing in the doorway. 'He said we could borrow his horse trailer if we want to,' Ray told the boys. 'He'd even come with us. It's a lot to ask, but. Maybe we'll think about it.' He strode into the middle of the sitting room, rubbing his hands together and grinning. 'The main thing is, we're on the way.' He punched at the air.

*

Matt heard Turbo before anyone else. He ran out to the track and waited as his mother got out of the car, then threw his arms around her and told her the news.

'So we know who the horse thief is, eh?' Matt's mother said as she slumped into a chair at the kitchen table and kicked off her shoes. Matt climbed onto her lap. Nick stood behind, his hand resting on the back of the chair. 'The chase is on, then.' She sounded tired, and not nearly as excited as the boys had hoped.

'Yep,' Ray replied. 'Want a beer?'

'Got something to celebrate, have we?' Mary sighed and nodded.

Ray grabbed a couple of beers from the refrigerator. He twisted the lids off and handed one to his wife. 'Where's Jaz? I thought she was coming over with you?'

'She'll be here soon.'

Ray frowned. 'She's not with that good-for-nothing?'

'She knows what she's doing,' his wife replied.

'Like hell she does!'

'I said she'll be here soon. Just leave it.'

Ray took a swig at his bottle. 'Whatever,' he said. Then he sat down at the table and fell silent.

Mary looked back at Nick and smiled. 'How was school today?' she asked him. He shrugged. Then she gave Matt a squeeze. 'What about you?'

Matt screwed up his mouth. 'All right.' Then his eyes brightened. 'I think Simon Croft wants to be my friend. He's got a horse called Gonzo, same age as Elvis.

Says his dad could work on both horses.' Matt looked across at his father. 'When we steal Elvis back, that is.'

'We're not stealing him,' Ray said. 'He's ours.'

Soon they heard a car pull up at the front of the house. Mary eased Matt off her lap.

'Come on, everyone,' she said, a knowing grin at the corner of her lips. 'That'll be Jaz.'

Nick and Matt ran into the hall, but Ray stayed at the table.

'You too,' Mary insisted as she strode from the kitchen. Ray rolled his eyes and scraped his chair back from the table.

Jaz and her boyfriend were at the front gate. Matt and Nick went to stand close to their sister, the younger boy taking hold of her hand.

'Hello, Mrs Turner,' the boyfriend said, waiting at the gate.

'Craig,' Mary nodded, glancing back at her husband. He hung in the doorway, staring at the verandah boards. 'Nice to see you.' There was a brief silence.

'This is Craig,' Jaz said, staring directly at her father. 'Dad!'

Ray glanced up. 'We've met,' he said. 'What's he doing here?'

Mary stiffened and glared at him.

'He's got something you might be interested in, Dad,' Jaz continued.

'Aw yeah?' Ray tilted his head at the youth.

Craig shoved his hands into his pockets and shifted from one foot to the other. 'Jaz said you needed a horse trailer,' he said, looking up at Ray.

'Did she?'

'Well, I've got one.' Craig stepped back, nodding towards his car.

'A horse trailer?' Ray craned his neck from the verandah, but couldn't see much in the dark.

Craig cleared his throat. 'More or less.'

The Turner family followed Craig through the gate. The boys hurried, but Ray took his time. Everyone stopped and stared at Craig's horse trailer. Hooked behind the blotchy green car was what looked like a heap of scrap metal.

'Needs a bit of work,' Craig said.

Ray kicked one of the wheels, and the trailer shuddered. 'You're not wrong,' he muttered.

'But Jaz says you're good at that sort of thing,' Craig added.

'Does she now?' Ray glanced at his daughter.

'And I can get hold of a welder for the weekend. If you're interested, that is.'

Ray stared at the trailer for a while longer. 'Yeah,' he replied eventually, trying to sound casual. 'We could be interested.'

chapter twenty-five

That weekend, the horse trailer was rebuilt. Ray rummaged through the back shed, and amongst his wrecks, for bits and pieces that might be of use. He also sent Matt and Nick scavenging far under the house.

Rust patches in the trailer were cut out and filled. Twisted panels were straightened, old joins strengthened, buckled bits bashed into shape. Ray decided to replace the axle entirely with one that he'd pulled off an old Jeep. It was too long, but Craig cut out a piece and welded it back together.

'Not bad,' Ray muttered as they stood back to inspect the job.

'Haven't finished yet,' Craig replied. 'You won't even see the join when I'm done.'

'Where'd you learn to weld like that?'

'Taught myself.'

The only tyres they had were bald, but that was the best they could do. The rusted mudguards were replaced, and the back ramp completely rebuilt using thick slabs of timber from under the house.

'I hope you don't expect me to lift that,' Mary said when she and Jaz appeared with morning tea on the Sunday.

'It just looks heavy, love,' Ray replied, reaching for the plate of scones with jam and cream.

Mary slapped his hand. 'Guests first, if you don't mind,' she said, and offered the plate to Craig. 'Tea?'

'Yes, please, Mrs Turner.' Craig smiled and bit into a scone. 'These are tops,' he mumbled.

'Must be your pretty face,' Ray sighed as he took a couple of scones. 'They never feed me like this.'

Matt and Nick painted the trailer, using a mixture of colours. The tin of green house paint only reached halfway, so Ray added bits of grey and brown he found in the spare-parts shed. And Matt discovered some yellow as well.

'Looks like an army vehicle,' Nick said when they finished.

Matt grinned. 'They won't see us coming, anyway.'

By Sunday afternoon the trailer was ready. They took it for a test run behind Turbo along the gravel track. Ray drove, with Craig beside him. Matt and Nick rode in the trailer. It rattled, and had a constant low squeal in the axle, but Ray was confident it would do the job.

'Ready to rock-and-roll.' Back at the house, Ray clapped his hands together, giving the trailer's wheels a kick. 'Talk about solid.' He slung his arm around Nick's shoulder.

Craig circled the trailer, tightening bolts.

'We're coming to get you, Elvis!' Matt yelled, climbing onto the mudguard.

'Look out, Mr Barnes,' Ray added with a grin. He rubbed Matt's hair and gave Nick a punch on the arm. For a moment it looked as though he was even going to slap Craig on the back.

'Speaking of Mr Barnes,' Craig said, pointing his spanner down the gravel road at the approaching lime-green car. 'Here come the spies right now.'

Mary Turner eyed off the horse trailer as she stepped out of Craig's car. She and Jaz had just made their second inspection of the Barnes's place. They'd been out on the Saturday as well. 'So this is the war machine,' she said. 'Does it go?'

'What sort of a question is that?' her husband scoffed.

'Like a bought one, Mum.' Matt leapt down from the mudguard. 'Did you see Elvis this time?'

'Looks pretty heavy,' Mary added. 'How's Turbo cope?'

Matt tugged at his mother's hand. 'Mum!'

'Don't worry about it,' Ray replied. The trailer, with its massive ramp, was heavy and Turbo would struggle, but Ray didn't need his wife telling him that. 'How'd you get on?'

'They've got loads of dogs,' Mary said. 'More than we saw yesterday.' Then she let herself be distracted by Matt's persistent tugging. 'Yes, Matty. We did see Elvis.'

Matt pushed close to his mother as she knelt beside him. 'Was he okay?'

When Jaz and Mary drove past the Barnes's farm, Frank and his son were trying to lead Elvis out of a small yard. The colt had reared back, and Frank's son had struck at him with a cane.

'He's not too bad,' Mary said, squeezing Matt's shoulder. 'We only just caught a glimpse of him. The dogs barked like mad when we slowed down, so we couldn't hang about for long.'

'Great,' Ray groaned. 'How are we supposed to sneak in with a bunch of yelping dogs?'

'They're pretty thin and hungry, Dad,' Jaz said. 'Maybe if we fed them, they'd keep quiet.'

Craig leant over Jaz's shoulder. 'I can get some bones and reject meat from the abattoir,' he suggested.

'Bring it over this evening,' Ray said at once.

'Where are they keeping Elvis?' Nick asked.

'There's a set of stables near the dogs,' his mother replied.

'When we drove back past the farm,' Jaz added, 'I think they were heading for those with Elvis.'

'You think?' Ray said.

'Well, it makes sense, Dad.'

'But you didn't actually see them put Elvis there?'

'We could hardly hang about, could we?' Mary replied. 'I mean, Craig's car doesn't exactly blend into the background, Ray, in case you haven't noticed. As it is, old Barnes might have seen us, anyway.'

Ray shook his head. 'Jeez!'

Matt turned to Jaz. 'Elvis was all right, wasn't he?'

Jaz didn't tell her little brother that the colt looked frightened and that the men had struck him several times. 'He still had plenty of go, Matt. I think I heard him whinny as we drove past.'

Matt's face brightened. 'He might've known it was you.'

'He might've, too, that's right.'

Nick patted his brother on the back. 'I reckon he knows you're coming to save him, Matty.'

Matt smiled. 'Yeah!'

'I still say we should park the trailer a little way from the house,' Matt's mother insisted, the annoyance growing in her voice. 'There's a dip in the road, where we wouldn't be seen by the Barnes.'

'You sure?' Ray asked.

'Sure as I can be!' Mary replied.

Ray shook his head. 'We'll have to lead him along the road. There could be traffic.'

'I know that!' Mary snapped. 'I have thought about it, Ray!' She glared at her husband. 'Why don't you go and have a bloody look for yourself?'

Mary turned to walk away, then felt a hand tugging at her sleeve. Matt pushed between his parents.

'Elvis knows we're coming!' he grinned up at them.

We'd built a boat! Our very own boat! Not just a raft strung together with rope. It leaked and it creaked and the sails were worn, but that didn't matter. We were ready to push out to sea, to beat the wind and the waves.

chapter twenty-six

At midnight they were ready.

Matt's mother made him lie down and try to sleep straight after tea. But he tossed about, bubbling with nerves. He imagined the colt running towards him, whinnying. He saw himself throwing his arms around Elvis's neck. But then he thought of the dogs barking, of Mr Barnes and his son waking and catching them.

He's a nasty piece of work, Frank Barnes, Mr Croft had said. I wouldn't put anything past him.

Twice Matt climbed out of bed and joined the others in the sitting room. Each time his mother led him back and stayed with him. The second time she lay down, too, and he snuggled into her arms.

*

'Go on,' Ray said, pushing his hand towards his wife's face. 'Put some on.'

The family was assembled in the kitchen. Everyone was dressed in their darkest clothes: black T-shirts or skivvies, and jeans. Ray had rubbed car grease on his face, and was trying to get the others to do the same. Matt and Nick did, and Craig was persuaded eventually, but Jaz and her mother refused.

They took both cars. Jaz went with Craig in his lime-green machine. Matt, Nick and their parents took Turbo, towing the horse trailer. At the last minute, Guts and TriHard jumped into the back seat with the boys. Ray didn't realise the dogs were there until they were pulling out onto the main road.

'Chuck 'em out,' he snarled. The dogs cringed on the back floor.

'They're all right, Dad,' Nick said. 'We'll watch them.'

Ray huffed and accelerated. 'Anyone else want a lift?' he yelled out the window. 'Any cows out there? Birds, pigs, cats? Elephants?' The boys laughed, but Mary rolled her eyes.

They hadn't gone far before Turbo's roar became even louder.

'Bloody muffler. Must be loose,' Ray grumbled,

turning to his wife. 'What have you been doing to poor old Turbo over in Grayston?'

'It's always been the car from hell. Don't blame me!'

'I had it purring, I did, before you got your hands on it.'

'Dream on.'

*

They were still arguing as they drove past the Barnes's place. The house, sitting close to the road, was in darkness. Ray slowed down, checking out the machinery shed behind the house, then pointing at the set of stables near the dog kennels.

'That's where you think Elvis is?' he said.

'Yes,' Mary replied curtly. 'To the best of my knowledge.'

Ray kept driving, following Craig to the place where they could turn the car and trailer, and where they were to meet for last minute plans.

'Now, you all know your jobs,' Ray said when they were gathered at the edge of the road. 'You did bring the meat, didn't you Craig?'

'Sure thing, Mr T.'

The plan was simple. They would park at the dip in the road just beyond the Barnes's house. Nick and his mother would let the ramp down, ready for Elvis, while the other four would sneak along to the house, find Elvis and bring him back.

'We'll only get one go at this,' Ray warned everyone as they stood in the dark. 'So let's do it right!' He thumped his fist at the night.

They leapt into the cars. Craig's started at once, but Turbo chugged and spluttered before firing. Ray turned onto the road.

'Hang on, Dad,' Nick called out. 'The dogs.'

It took ten minutes to find Guts and TriHard. They'd wandered off into a nearby paddock. TriHard had jumped into a dam, and returned covered in mud. Guts had found a dead sheep.

'They'll smell us coming.' Ray groaned as they finally drove back along the road. Two of the passenger windows in Turbo had always been jammed shut, and the driver's window only opened half-way.

'What kept you?' Craig whispered into Ray's window. 'Pooh!' He quickly pulled back.

'Don't ask,' Ray said.

Four dark figures, two of them some distance ahead of the others, crept along the edge of the road towards the old farmhouse. As they drew closer to the house, the leading pair paused. Then they moved on, through the front gate and past the house towards the dog kennels. There was some barking, but that soon stopped, and then the first two figures crept through the shadows to a car parked next to the house. The other pair slid towards the stables.

Another two dark shapes were also moving along the road towards the Barnes's house. One of them made a clanking sound as it walked.

'Around the back,' Ray whispered to Matt. 'That's where Mum said he is.'

But there was no Elvis. Two other horses snorted when Matt and his father peered into the stables. But the last stall was empty.

'Damn. They must've put him somewhere else.'

By now, Jaz and Craig had finished with the car, and came silently to join the others. Craig displayed the distributor cable with a grin.

'He's not there!' Ray whispered.

Matt held up his hand to keep the others quiet.

'Elvis,' he called softly, knowing that if the colt was nearby he would reply. They stood motionless, straining to listen. Matt called again. A dog barked from the kennels—a familiar bark, Ray couldn't help thinking. He also heard a clanking sound that he knew only too well. But there was another sound. Very soft. Almost like a laugh.

'Over there,' Craig pointed to the machinery shed.

'They're bolted,' Ray cursed. The double corrugated-iron doors were secured by chain and padlock. Behind the doors they could hear a shuffling sound, then the muffled call of a horse. 'Look for an iron bar or something, bolt cutters maybe.'

'Elvis,' Matt murmured through the gap between the doors. The colt nickered. 'We'll get you out soon.' Elvis whinnied, and this time several dogs barked.

A moment later Craig appeared with a steel dropper he'd found in a pile at the side of the shed. He slipped it through the chain. He and Ray twisted the dropper. The clanking of the broken chain brought more barking, and then when the large doors creaked loudly open, the dogs exploded. They were fighting, and amongst the snarling was a high-pitched yelp the Turners knew only too well.

'Guts!' Ray whispered to the others. 'Him and TriHard are fighting with Barnes's dogs! Bloody hell!'

A light flicked on in the house. A muffled voice shouted from one of the rooms. 'Shut up, ya mongrels!'

'Hurry!' Ray insisted. Elvis was right at the doorway. He shuffled forward, pushing his face against Matt. 'He's hobbled! Get 'em off, quick!' Matt fumbled at the stiff buckles, but with no success. Another light in the house. The dogs went berserk.

'Hang on!' Craig groped in his pockets and produced a pen knife. He leaned down and, with a flash of his knife, slit the leather hobbles. 'Let's go!'

Frank Barnes poked his head out the bedroom window at the side of the house to yell at the dogs, just in time to see four people and a colt scramble out through the front gate.

'Get the gun!' he shouted.

More lights came on in the house, then on the verandah. Frank stumbled out in his pyjamas, followed by his son with a shotgun. The son fumbled two shells into the breach and fired into the air. Two dogs scurried out the gate and clanked away into the dark.

'In the car!' Frank Barnes shouted. 'We'll run 'em down!'

Mary heard the barking, then the shots. She left Nick at the ramp, climbed into Turbo, and started the car. Nick shifted nervously from one foot to the other. Then he saw the scramble of horse and people coming towards him. Another shot, followed by the unmistakeable clank of TriHard.

'In the trailer with him,' Ray shouted. 'Quick!' He gripped the lead rope and began pulling the colt towards the ramp.

But Elvis knew about horse trailers and trucks. As soon as he saw the ramp he pulled back. Ray tugged harder, while Craig and Nick and Jaz gathered behind the colt, pushing him.

Matt watched them struggling.

'Not like that!' he yelled. Elvis couldn't be forced. The shouting and shoving would only make him fight more.

Ray pulled harder. They could hear the Barnes's car engine turning over and over. Before long the two men would give up on the car and come after them on foot. Ray swore, and tugged on the rope, but the colt reared back.

Matt stepped onto the ramp and grabbed the rope from his father. 'Let me do it,' he insisted.

Matt let the rope slacken at once, and reached towards Elvis. The colt was trembling. Matt whispered in his ear as he ran his hands over him.

'It's me, Elvis. Come on, mate,' he said softly. 'We've got to do this.'

The colt sniffed at the boy, then gradually stopped fidgeting.

'You and me.' Matt turned his back and walked up the ramp, pretending to ignore Elvis, leaving the rope hanging loosely.

Elvis stared at the boy's back. He lowered his head, snorted at the ramp, struck at it several times with a front hoof.

'Come on, come on!' his father urged from the side of the ramp.

'Dad!' Jaz hissed. 'Let him do it.'

'We've got to hurry!'

Matt glanced sideway at his father. 'He'll come if we wait,' he whispered. 'But he'll never come if we try to force him.' Matt took another step and waited with his back to the horse.

Elvis tossed his head and glanced around at the others. They were poised, motionless, waiting. The colt looked back at the boy and stepped onto the ramp.

Ray stared in the direction of the Barnes's house. The car had stopped chugging. A pause, and then a different engine started turning over. The truck! Ray clenched his fists—we forgot about the truck!—his throat dry. Mary gripped the steering wheel. Nick closed his eyes and crossed his fingers. Jaz squeezed Craig's hand. Matt made a soft clicking sound with his mouth.

The colt pricked his ears and stared over his shoulder towards the farm house and the sound of the truck. He took another two steps.

Matt walked slowly into the trailer. 'It's okay, Elvis,' he said quietly. 'Come on.'

The colt banged on the ramp with his front hoofs, then stretched his nose into the trailer. He could hear the rattle of the truck as it pulled out of the shed. They could all hear it.

'Just keep coming, Elvis.' The boy's voice was gentle as he edged into the trailer. 'A few more steps.'

Elvis sniffed the sides, snorted again, then clattered up the last bit of the ramp and joined the boy. Matt hugged him as the others darted forward to heave up the ramp, bolting boy and horse inside.

'Go, go, go!' Ray shouted.

chapter twenty-seven

Nick and his father ripped open Turbo's doors and leapt in. Jaz and Craig jumped into their car and pulled onto the road with the wheels spinning. Mary revved Turbo before clunking it into gear. But as she eased the clutch out, the old car suddenly began to splutter.

'Turbo!' Ray growled. 'Don't do this to me!'

He pounded the windscreen and thumped the dashboard with his fists. The dusty white truck turned out of the farm onto the road. Turbo backfired, sent out a cloud of exhaust fumes, and at last the engine engaged with a roar. The car pulled onto the road just as the truck loomed out of the dark behind them.

'The dogs!' Nick suddenly yelled.

Guts and TriHard were running along beside the car. Mary slowed down.

'Keep going!' Ray shouted.

He opened his door and yelled at the dogs. 'Hurry up, you useless flea-taxis. Get up in here!' Guts leapt, scrabbling with his claws as Ray hauled him over the front seat into the back of the car. TriHard was not so fast, and couldn't quite make the jump. Mary slowed a little while Ray hung out the side of Turbo and grabbed the dog by the collar, dragging him in.

'Remind me not to bring these two next time we steal a horse,' he said.

They came to a long hill. Turbo began to slow down, the truck gaining on them. Mary pressed on the accelerator, but Turbo only roared louder. Then a dreadful racket erupted from underneath the car. The muffler had become detached. It dragged along the road, screeching and scraping and sending out sparks, before eventually breaking off and clattering under the trailer. The truck swerved, but drove over the top of it.

Matt watched the truck grumbling closer, its headlights like big burning eyes. He clutched onto Elvis's mane, arms around the colt's neck, hugging close, hiding behind him.

'Put your bloody foot down, woman!' Ray shouted.

'I can't put it down any further!' Mary yelled back.

'It's not a funeral! Give it some juice, can't you, for Chrisake!'

'Don't shout at me!'

The truck kept drawing nearer.

'Well, get a move on, then!'

'You and your lousy, pathetic ideas!' Mary shouted.

'You and your fancy-pants boyfriend!' Ray yelled back.

'Your stinking dogs and your crap heap of car!'

'Crap heap, eh? Didn't stop you driving it!'

'Jeez, Ray! I wish I'd never let you talk me into this mess!'

'Aw, quit your whingeing, and drop into second gear, or we really *will* be in a mess!'

Mary shoved a tape into the cassette player and turned the volume up full. Ray grabbed at the volume knob, but his wife tore it off and tossed it over her shoulder. Then she ripped the gear stick into second and flattened her foot to the floor.

Turbo coughed, roared, and then gradually began to pull away from the truck.

Nick pressed himself into the back seat, and the dogs cringed on the floor, as the parents continued shouting above the King and the roar of the car. When Turbo reached the crest of the hill, the truck had fallen well behind. Mary changed to third gear and accelerated again. The car gathered speed on the long downhill stretch, the trailer rattling and wobbling behind.

Matt sighed with relief as he watched the truck's headlights shrink and then vanish beyond the crest of the hill. He felt the thick horse hairs tangled between his fingers, and realised how tightly he'd been clutching Elvis's mane.

Our ramshackle boat shuddered and groaned as it shot down the face of a wave. It lurched and tilted, the bow dipping deep, almost engulfed by the surge.

*

Sergeant Jenkins heard them coming. He didn't usually sit in his car on the Grayston road at two in the morning. But he hadn't been able to sleep, so he'd gone for a drive. He was parked in a picnic spot a few kilometres from Werrawee, enjoying the night air, when he heard the thunder of the car. He listened carefully. There was shouting, too, as the car and horse trailer shot past. And his favourite Elvis Presley song.

Ray and Mary both spotted the police car at the same time. They stopped shouting, stared at each other and cursed. The police car was soon behind them, flashing its headlights. Mary pressed her foot on the brake, the trailer swaying, and pulled over to the side of the road. She switched off the ignition. The King died instantly. Turbo coughed, backfired, and eventually fell silent too. Ray and Mary stared straight ahead.

Nick sat up and looked back as Sergeant Jenkins stepped from his car and strolled towards them.

'Jeez, Mum,' he said. 'You're in for it now.'

Ray and Mary said nothing. All that could be heard was the clumping of hoofs in the trailer.

Sergeant Jenkins leaned on the side of the car and peered in at Mary. 'I thought it was you lot.' He craned his neck to see Nick and the dogs in the back. 'Pooh! You got a dead body in there?' He wrinkled his nose and stepped back from the car. 'Where's young Matty, then?'

'In the back,' Mary replied.

The sergeant peered through the back window.

'Right in the back,' Mary added.

'In the boot?' the sergeant asked.

'In the trailer.'

'You're kidding.'

The Turners shook their heads at the sergeant. He strolled to the back of the horse trailer and looked over the ramp. First he saw the colt's rump and shoulders, and then noticed the boy's face peering from behind the young horse's neck.

'That you, Matty?'

'Yes, Sergeant Jenkins.'

The sergeant shook his head. 'Morning, Elvis,' he added as the colt craned his neck to peer back at him. Then Sergeant Jenkins returned to the car. Ray and Mary had got out and were leaning against the bonnet.

'I'll have to fine you, of course,' he said, pulling his book from his pocket.

'What for?' Ray asked.

'Where do you want me to start?'

'Look. If it's the trailer, we were going to register it tomorrow. Today, I mean. Weren't we, luv?' Ray nudged his wife.

'Absolutely,' she agreed. 'Ray's got all the papers ready. He's very good with that sort of thing.'

'I'm sure he is,' Sergeant Jenkins smiled and opened his book. He was about to begin writing when a truck came hurtling around the corner, skidding to a halt behind the police car.

Two men jumped out.

'You've got them!' yelled Frank Barnes. 'Who says the police are no good?'

'I don't know,' Sergent Jenkins lowered his notebook. 'Who *does* say the police are no good?'

'Not me, that's for sure,' said Ray. 'They're an essential part of the community.'

'Me neither,' added Mary. 'Must've been you, Mr Barnes.'

Frank Barnes scowled. 'Arrest them, Sergeant!'

'Hang on.' Sergeant Jenkins puffed out his chest. 'I decide who gets arrested around here.'

'They've stolen my horse.'

'Your horse?'

'Yeah! They trespassed onto my farm, broke into my shed, and stole my horse. It's there, in the trailer.'

Sergeant Jenkins sauntered across to the side of the trailer and gazed in.

'I can't see any horse,' he said.

Frank Barnes marched over. 'There!' he said. 'Right in front of your nose.'

'That's no horse,' the sergeant said. 'That's Elvis. A Living Legend!'

'What are you talking about? They've stolen my horse and I want them charged. Now!'

'Hold on a tick. I think you've got things a bit mixed up.' The sergeant took Frank Barnes by the arm, led him away from the trailer, and then gazed back at the Turners.

Ray and Mary were still leaning against Turbo. Ray wiped as much grease from his face as he could and put his arm around Mary. The two of them smiled across at the sergeant as though for a happy snap.

'What we have here is a fine family out for a Sunday drive. Monday morning drive, anyway. Mum and Dad and the two kids, even got their pets along with them for the ride. I would have called this a picture of perfect family harmony.'

Nick and the dogs had clambered into the front seat, and were poking their heads out of the window. Matt pulled himself up and gazed over the side of the trailer.

'Yep,' the sergeant nodded. 'Family harmony. That's what I see.'

Elvis's tail was flashing above the ramp.

'And then you turn up! Speeding in a truck with tyres that are as bald as I am.'

'They're not that bald,' Frank Barnes's son protested.

'Watch it, boy!' the sergeant growled, and then turned back to Frank. 'You leap out of your truck, behave in a rude and aggressive manner, and then have the audacity to tell me how to do my job!' He made a show of opening his notebook again. 'Now I suggest you and your son get back in your truck and disappear. Unless, of course, you want to pursue this matter further.' The sergeant raised his pen. 'Back at the station.'

Frank Barnes and his son did as the sergeant suggested.

chapter twenty-eight

Jaz and Craig were waiting anxiously at the front of the house.

'What happened to you lot?' Jaz asked as the car doors flew open and her parents clambered out, followed by Nick and the dogs.

'We were gunna come back and look for you,' Craig said.

Ray grinned, showing the gap in his top front teeth. 'You would've got a good laugh if you had,' he said, striding to the back of the ramp. Matt's head appeared over the side of the trailer and Elvis nickered. 'Tell you all about it when we get the King and the kid out of this contraption.'

Once the heavy ramp was lowered, Matt gently pressed Elvis's chest until the colt began stepping backwards. Elvis paused on the ramp, looking over his shoulder.

'Ladies and gentlemen,' Ray said, holding his hand

to his mouth like a microphone. 'Here he is! The guy you've all been waiting for. The one and only . . . Elvis!'

The colt clattered down the ramp, Matt following with the lead rope in his hand. Ray began clapping, and the others followed. Elvis stared around at the circle of faces, his ears pricked, his eyes alert. He whinnied loudly, then began nibbling on a clump of grass at the edge of the ramp.

'Anyone for an early breakfast?' Mary asked.

'Pancakes, Mum?' said Matt.

Mary glanced at Jaz. 'I think we could manage that, couldn't we?'

'Caramel sauce on mine, thanks,' Ray said. 'Me and the boys will get this beast off Turbo's back. The old girl is gunna need a good rest after what she's been through.'

'And a new muffler,' Mary suggested.

*

Matt leant against the gatepost. The colt had finished his oats and hay, and was standing beside the boy, his head over the gate. Matt's fingers played with Elvis's mane, stroking the long thick hair as he gazed towards the house.

A broad beam of light shone from the kitchen into the back garden. Matt caught glimpses of his mother and sister preparing breakfast. Ray was standing between Nick and Craig near the clothes line, in the light from the kitchen window.

Nick laughed. 'You should have seen their faces when the sergeant told them to get going!'

'Old Frank was furious!' Ray said.

'I reckon we've seen the last of those two, eh, Dad?' Nick added.

'Too right, we have. Now that me and the sarge are like that.' Ray held up two crossed fingers.

Matt's mother appeared at the back door carrying a tray piled with food. 'Don't believe a word he says,' she shouted. Jaz followed with another tray.

Ray raced Nick and Craig to the back steps.

Mary peered towards Elvis's pen. 'Come on, Matty,' she called. 'You'll have to be quick with this pack of horse thieves if you want any pancakes.'

Matt opened the gate and stepped through, closing it quickly before Elvis could follow. 'I'll save you some,' he whispered to the colt, rubbing his forehead briskly. Then he sprinted to the house.

They ate their breakfast sitting on the edge of the verandah with their legs dangling over.

Matt kept a piece of pancake for Elvis. But he didn't get to take it to him. He was too sleepy. He lay his head on his mother's lap and stared towards Elvis's pen. As his eyes drooped shut, he heard the colt's soft, reassuring call through the dark.

'I'll give Jimmy Croft a call in the morning,' Ray said as he carried Matt to his bedroom.

Mary tucked Matt into bed. 'Good idea,' she said, leaning down and kissing her son.

The picture book was poking out from under the pillow. Mary drew it out, glanced at the cover, smiled to herself, then slid it back.

Ray and Mary paused at the bedroom door, looking at the small bundle in the bed.

Ray chuckled. 'Did you hear what Sergeant Jenkins said?'

'What about?'

'About us,' Ray replied. His wife shook her head. 'A picture of perfect family harmony.'

'You must have been dreaming,' Mary said.

After they'd gone, Matt opened his eyes. Taking the picture book from under his pillow, he climbed out of bed and, rummaging beneath it, pulled out a cardboard box almost filled with old toys. Peering at the book in the half light, he could just make out the figure of the boy on the beach. He slid his fingers over the picture, across the boy, onto the sand, and down to the edge of the sea. Then he placed the book in the box and pushed it back under the bed.

Epilogue

There are some things you can never throw away.
You keep them in a box at the back of your mind,
and let them surface from time to time.

I'll never forget those first few months when Elvis
lived with us. If he hadn't come into my life, I might
still be standing on the shore, staring out to sea.
Either that, or I'd be floundering about
in the water, slowly sinking.

Elvis helped me face up to the wind and the waves,
the sharks and the tentacles, the tremors, the storms.
He helped me feel at home in the sea,
and leave my island behind.

And for a brief time he showed us
all how to swim together.

738 A8 F$ 7797
10/09/06 44200